Copyright © 2011 by Quirk Productions, Inc.
WORST-CASE SCENARIO ® is a registered trademark of Quirk Productions, Inc.

**Visit www.worstcasescenarios.com to learn more about the series.**

Library of Congress Cataloging-in-Publication Data available.
ISBN 978-0-8118-7123-5

Book design by Eloise Leigh and Mark Neely.
Typeset in Akzidenz-Grotesk Std.

Manufactured by C & C Offset Longgang, Shenzhen, China, in December 2010.

10 9 8 7 6 5 4 3 2 1

This product conforms to CPSIA 2008.

Chronicle Books LLC
680 Second Street, San Francisco, California 94107
www.chroniclekids.com

Image credits: Page 189: (airport) Christopher Howey/Dreamstime.com; (Namche Bazaar) Granitepeaker/Dreamstime.com; (yak) Andre Wroblewski/Dreamstime.com; (bridge) Steve Estvanik/Dreamstime.com. Page 190: David Morton. Page 191: (prayer wheels) Shariff Che Lah/Dreamstime.com. Page 194: (axe) Mcech/Dreamstime.com; (boot) David Morton. Page 195: (goggles): Brad Calkins/Dreamstime.com; (glacier glasses) David Morton. All other photos: Shutterstock.com.

# The
# WORST-CASE SCENARIO

## ULTIMATE ADVENTURE

# EVEREST

## YOU DECIDE HOW TO SURVIVE!

By Bill Doyle and David Borgenicht
with David Morton, climbing consultant

*Illustrated by Yancey Labat*

chronicle books · san francisco

# EVEREST ADVENTURE

YOU are about to join the youngest team ever to climb the tallest mountain on the planet. But will you reach the summit and set a new world record?

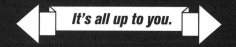

*It's all up to you.*

At many points in this action-packed adventure, you'll be given choices—and the decisions you make will change the course of your story.

There are twenty-six possible endings to your Everest expedition. Some are *almost* victories; some are disasters. But only ONE ROUTE through the book will get you triumphantly to the summit and back down in one piece. Can you make all the right choices to achieve the ultimate success?

**Before you start, make sure to read the Expedition File at the back of the book, starting on page 187.** It has the tips and information you'll need to make smart choices.

Advice from your guides will also help you along the way. But most of all, listen to your gut, and trust that YOU have the wise judgment and good instincts you'll need to make it to the top of the world!

# YOUR TEAM

**CLIMBERS**

## GARRETT SCOTT
*AGE: 13*
*HOME COUNTRY: AUSTRALIA*

Growing up in Sydney, Garrett was the class clown—until his parents introduced him to climbing as a way to soak up some of that wild energy. He loved it. While still the jokester among friends, Garrett wants to be taken seriously as a climber—so badly that he might take one too many risks on the mountain.

## JULIA REYEZ
*AGE: 13*
*HOME COUNTRY: ARGENTINA*

A city girl from Buenos Aires, Julia has been climbing with her mom and dad for years. Only one thing can stand in her way on this expedition—and that's herself. She has a secret problem that pops up when she reaches high altitudes. And since Everest is all about altitude, that could mean trouble.

**CLIMBER**

## HANS MOSER
*AGE: 27  HOME COUNTRY: SWITZERLAND*

A true pro and always deadly serious, Hans has already bagged many of the world's most impressive peaks—Makalu, K2, Denali, and more. Stuck in the shadow of his famous family of climbers, Hans thinks the only way to make a name for himself is to do something extreme—like climb Everest without a bottle of oxygen, even at the top where the air is dangerously thin.

## JAKE STAPLES
*AGE: 43   HOME COUNTRY: U.S.A.*

This wealthy owner of a famous video game company in Dallas is the major sponsor of the expedition. He's hired Hans Moser to be his personal guide on the trip and to give him climbing tips. Too bad Jake can insist on being in charge even when he doesn't exactly know what he's doing—and that may prove his downfall.

**CLIMBER**

## RUSS MORELLO
*AGE: 37*
*HOME COUNTRY: U.S.A.*

A lifelong climber and former marine, Russ grew up in the Pacific Northwest and first summited Everest fifteen years ago. After working as a guide for other expeditions, he started a trekking company with his wife. If you reach the summit, the press will help their business.
Does that mean he might be tempted to push you too hard?

## SUSAN "DOC" MORELLO
*AGE: 34*
*HOME COUNTRY: U.S.A.*

The expedition's worrywart and Russ's wife, Susan became a surfing champ while attending medical school in California. Now everyone just calls her Doc. Her climbing skills, medical know-how, and sharp instincts make her a real ace on the mountain—but you might discover that she can take her quest for caution too far.

**THE GUIDES**

## THE SHERPAS

The Sherpa people are an ethnic group from the mountains of Nepal. (Sherpa means "People of the East.") Famous for their great mountaineering skills, Sherpas are Buddhist, and they speak a language that's a dialect of Tibetan. They all use the last name "Sherpa."

There will be fifteen Sherpas on your expedition. Here are the two you will know best: the head Sherpa and the Sherpa who will be assigned to you. Your assigned Sherpa will help carry your gear and climb with you on summit day.

### DORJEE SHERPA
*AGE: 37   HOME COUNTRY: NEPAL*

A spiritual man, Dorjee ("Lightning Bolt") Sherpa is the trip's head Sherpa, or sirdar. An old friend of Doc and Russ's, he has the most experience of anyone on the expedition. While, of course, he wishes for the success of your expedition, he doubts the wisdom of allowing such young climbers to attempt to summit Everest.

### LHAKPA SHERPA
*AGE: 22   HOME COUNTRY: NEPAL*

Born the youngest of five into a family of farmers, Lhakpa Sherpa has dreamed of climbing Everest his entire life. On his two previous expeditions, he didn't make it to the summit. Now the two of you share the same dream: to reach the top of the world. But will his total lack of experience at the summit slow you down—or worse?

# THE ADVENTURE BEGINS...

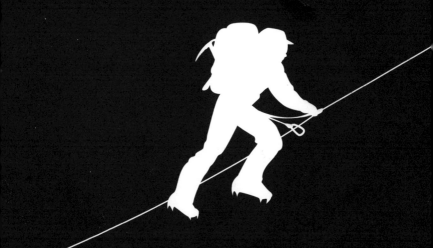

APRIL 1, 11:30 A.M.

IN THE SKY OVER LUKLA, NEPAL

"Fasten your seat belts for our final descent into Lukla!" the pilot shouts over the roaring engines of the tiny plane.

You and the six other passengers brace yourselves as the aircraft plunges toward Lukla, a small village deep in the Himalayan Mountains. The wind flicks the plane up and down like a toy, and with each crazy bounce, your stomach lets you know it's *not* enjoying the ride.

"Before we land," the pilot continues, "I'd like to wish good luck to our three brave young passengers. May you become the youngest team to ever summit Mount Everest!"

Even though you feel like you're about to throw up, you can't help grinning. After all, you're one of the "brave young passengers" the pilot is talking about. You've been training hard to make this dream come true. And finally you're here in Nepal, about to climb the world's tallest mountain.

You glance around the cramped cabin at the other members of your team. Across the aisle is Garrett Scott, a thirteen-year-old Australian kid. "Brave young passengers?" He laughs. "Thanks, mate!"

Next to Garrett is Julia Reyez, who's also thirteen. She's from Argentina. Though you just met Garrett and Julia in Kathmandu this morning, you like them both already.

You give Julia a thumbs-up, but the dark-haired Argentine doesn't notice. She's staring wide-eyed at something outside.

You look out the window too—and grip the armrest tightly. Tiny Lukla airport is approaching fast. This is the world's third-highest airport, and some say the most terrifying.

"That's the runway?" Jake Staples shouts behind you. "My driveway is longer than that!"

Jake is a sponsor of the expedition. Everest climbs are expensive, so you have many sponsors, but most of them just fork over money. Jake, the president of a big video game company, decided he wanted to climb with the team.

Next to Jake is Hans Moser, an expert climber from Switzerland. Jake hired Hans to help him train and to be his personal guide for the trip. Hans's icy blue eyes and weatherworn face make him look very serious. You have yet to see him crack a smile.

At the front of the plane is Russ Morello, your lead guide. He's an ex-marine who looks like he has the muscle power to climb Everest three times before breakfast. Across the aisle is his wife, Susan. She's an experienced guide, too, and the team doctor, which is why everyone just calls her Doc.

That's your team—these are the six people you'll hopefully be standing with on the top of the world. But first, you have to land!

Russ turns around to look at everyone and says, "The adventure starts here, folks! Hang on!"

The plane plummets toward Lukla, bouncing and shaking the whole time. Then—SCREECH!—the landing gear skids onto the airstrip. You grit your teeth as the plane screams down the runway and, finally, just before the short landing strip ends, jerks to a stop.

Jake lets out a Texas whoop. Julia pumps a fist in the air. And Garrett opens his mouth . . . and throws up all over his feet.

The stench fills the cabin.

"I warned you about that extra omelet at breakfast," Doc says, tossing a towel back to Garrett so he can clean himself up.

"Ah, Doc," Garrett laughs. "It's no big deal. After all, chunder happens!"

Luckily, that's when the pilot pops open the plane's door, letting in the crisp morning air. Even when you step out onto the airstrip and gaze at the mountain range ahead of you, it's hard to believe you're actually here in the middle of the Himalayas. You can't see Everest yet, but just the thrill of being so close makes you excited to get going.

Russ strides over to you. With one huge, muscular arm, he puts you in a friendly headlock. "So, 'brave young passenger,'" he teases, "are you ready to summit Everest?"

"Bring it on," you say in your action-hero voice.

It was Russ's idea to bring you, Garrett, and Julia together to climb Everest. Each of you has climbed at least one big peak with Russ and Doc before, and each of you e-mailed the couple last year to see if they'd guide you to the top of Everest.

Russ and Doc thought that you three were up to the challenge, and they figured, why not make it a world-record-setting expedition—the youngest team ever? You loved the

sound of that. Your family, well, they needed some convincing. But luckily, they decided they trusted Russ and Doc enough to let you go.

Everyone grabs backpacks and, after a quick cup of tea, Russ leads the way into Lukla. You head down a narrow street jammed with vendors selling clothing, yak cheese, and hiking gear.

It will take ten days of hiking through mountains and valleys to get to Everest Base Camp. You can't just fly there in a helicopter—you wish!—you have to walk there slowly, because your body needs time to get used to the altitude. The higher you go, the less oxygen there is to breathe. That kind of "thin air" can make you feel pretty awful—if you're not careful.

But you're not worried about that at this second. Now you're walking with your team, feeling strong, knowing that each step is taking you closer to Everest.

Soon you've left the village and find yourself on a sloping, stony path. The hike is mostly downhill and easygoing. You're loving the sunshine and the bright blue sky on this late spring day. As you take in the views of the mountainsides covered with rice fields and little cottages, you think, *This is incredible! I'm really here!* And then suddenly—

*Ummph.*

You bang into a wall. A very hairy, smelly wall.

It's a yak loaded down with cargo, being led up the hill by a local farmer.

"Making new friends?" Julia asks you with a laugh.

You're embarrassed but chuckle along with her. You notice Hans isn't laughing, though. Instead, the Swiss climber is shaking his head as if you've just made a huge mistake.

A few hours later, you arrive in the small village of Phakding. With the sun setting and the temperature falling, you're glad when Doc points out the three-story lodge up ahead. After dropping your things in your room, you return downstairs for a team dinner of "Yak Sizzler."

"Don't worry." Russ chuckles, seeing your weirded-out face. "The locals just call it that. They wouldn't kill yaks to eat—it's really water buffalo."

As if that's supposed to make you feel better!

Fortunately, the water buffalo steak is served with fries, which you love, and the meat is actually pretty good. After everyone eats, Russ says, "Tomorrow we'll climb our first big hill. And I want you all to take it easy. Don't push yourselves too hard, or you could get hurt. Now go get some sleep!"

Up in your room, as you're drifting off, you hear voices outside your window. It's Doc and Hans.

"Come on, Hans," Doc is saying. "Bumping into a yak isn't that big of a deal. I think—"

"A good climber is always alert and aware," Hans interrupts, his words cold and clipped. "And it's not just the mind I worry about with these three. They seem weak to me. Weak in the body. When I was their age . . ."

Their voices trail off as they head back inside the lodge. Now you're wide awake. Hearing Hans's doubts about you makes you question your climbing skills. That's something you've never done . . . until now, that is.

Finally, morning arrives. You share a quick breakfast with the team—eggs and pancakes, surprisingly like home—and head off. Russ leads you along the Dudh Kosi river gorge through several villages. You cross a bunch of narrow bridges that dangle over the river and wobble as you walk on them.

Then, in the afternoon, you find yourself standing at the bottom of a steep hill. A *very* steep hill.

"Whoa," you breathe. At the top is Namche Bazaar, the largest village in the Everest region.

Julia doesn't hesitate. "Well, what are you waiting for?" she asks, starting up at a fast pace.

"Let's go!" Garrett shouts and runs after her.

That's when the idea hits you. You could go full speed up Namche Hill and get to the top first. It could be a great way to crush any doubts that Hans—and now you—have about you being ready for Everest.

Do you do it?

**IF YOU LEAD THE CHARGE UP NAMCHE HILL, TURN TO PAGE 29.**

**IF YOU TAKE IT SLOW, TURN TO PAGE 25.**

"Okay," Jake says. "I get it!"

The two of you take your last rappel. As you make your way down, you keep an eye on Jake to make sure he's doing everything right.

Really, though, you should be paying attention to where you're going. Your foot comes down on a loose chunk of ice, and your leg twists out to the side.

There's a tiny *pop* in your knee.

*That didn't sound good.*

After you finish the rappel, you test out your knee. It hurts, but at least you can stand and walk. When you tell Jake what happened, he shrugs. "No pain, no gain, right?"

*Thanks for the sympathy.*

You hobble back to Base Camp. When you finally arrive, the sun is setting. The day was pretty miserable—and it might get worse if you tell Doc about your knee. She and Russ will let you have it for sneaking off to the icefall. Maybe you can just deal with the pain. After all, you can still walk on it.

**IF YOU TELL DOC ABOUT SNEAKING OFF WITH JAKE AND HURTING YOUR KNEE, TURN TO PAGE 85.**

**IF YOU KEEP QUIET, TURN TO PAGE 39.**

That night at midnight, you sit up in bed, feeling like someone just punched you in the gut.

*Oh, man. I'm going to hurl.*

You rush down the hall to the bathroom. Someone's inside and Hans is waiting in line. He takes one look at you and asks, "What did you eat? Something bad?"

The answer pops in your head: *The apple pie.*

No wonder the locals weren't eating it!

You rush down the lodge stairs as fast as you can and dash outside into the darkness, looking for a place to throw up. You stumble on a rock and fall—*Crack! Crack!*

Both your wrists snap back. Lying there, you turn your head to throw up. Could it get any worse?

Doc rushes to your side—Hans must have told her you were sick—and says, "You've broken both wrists. You can't possibly climb like this."

The next morning, as Doc starts the hike back to Lukla airport with you, the other team members are there to see you off. Your trip is over. And, with two busted wrists, you can't even wave good-bye.

**THE END**

Slowly and steadily, you hike up Namche Hill. You're amazed as local porters pass you by. They're carrying loads twice their size on their backs and wearing thin-soled shoes, and yet they walk right past you and never stop. You, on the other hand, make lots of stops to catch your breath.

On one of your breaks, you look into the distance—and gasp. There it is. Mount Everest. This is your first peek of the mountain. Even though clumps of trees block much of the view, you're thrilled to see it in person and not just in a book or online.

You tear your eyes away and continue on. To your surprise, you catch up with Julia and Garrett halfway up the hill. Russ has stopped to check on the two teens. Garrett's bent over, like he might throw up again. Breathing heavily, Julia is still climbing—but barely.

"You guys okay?" you ask.

Julia waves weakly and Garrett slowly nods. You ask if they saw Everest, but they grunt a disappointed no. They were too busy pounding up the trail.

"Nice work," Russ pats your back as you hike by. "You took it nice and slow."

You finally reach the top where Hans and Jake are waiting. The Swiss climber is shaking his head as he watches Julia and Garrett struggle below. But Jake shouts encouragement: "Come on, you two! Let's finish this thing so we can get some grub!"

As everyone finishes the climb, you take your first look at Namche Bazaar and its low stone buildings that spread out up the mountainside. You'll be staying here for two nights as your body slowly churns out extra red blood cells and, little by little, adjusts to being up so high.

"Here," Doc says, pushing a bottle of water into your hands. "It's easy to get dehydrated at this altitude."

You don't want to admit it, but even though you climbed slowly, you're not feeling so great. There's a dull ache in the back of your skull. By the time you get to the lodge and up to your room, that ache is more like a sharp hammering.

You put your head down on your pillow, determined to take just a quick nap. But when you open your eyes again, the sun is rising. You slept through the night into the next day! But at least your headache's gone.

You head downstairs and find Garrett and Julia. Garrett says, "Our fearless leader Russ wants the team to meet him for an early lunch at eleven o'clock. He says we have to try the best *dal bhat* in Namche Bazaar."

"We've got an hour until lunch," Julia says. "We're going to take a quick look around town. Want to come?"

As if on cue, your stomach growls. Loudly.

"I think your belly just answered for you," Garrett says. "Let's go."

Namche Bazaar is much bigger than you thought, with stores selling food, clothes, farming supplies, climbing gear, and souvenirs like Everest T-shirts and pins. There are even several bakeries selling apple pies and cinnamon rolls. The smell is amazing.

After you've walked around a bit, Julia points to an Internet cafe. You're pretty impressed to see computers in a mountain village where there aren't even any roads or cars.

"Let's stop in there. I can update my blog," Julia says.

"No time," Garrett responds, tapping his watch. "The Internet is really slow here."

Julia arches an eyebrow. "I'm sorry? Are you describing the Internet or your climb yesterday?"

"*Hmm,*" Garrett says, laughing. "I could've sworn that was you wheezing on the hill right next to me."

Just then your stomach moans again. It'd be great to fill up on something fast. But you don't want to be late for the lunch with the team. That'd probably be just what Hans would expect.

At a teahouse restaurant nearby, you see locals sitting down to small metal trays filled with mounds of different kinds of food.

"That's *dal bhat*," Julia says, following your gaze. "It's lentils and rice, with vegetables on the side. Locals might eat it two or three times a day."

Rice, lentils, and something green that looks like spinach first thing in the morning? You wonder if your stomach needs time to adjust to local food, just like your body has to adjust to the altitude.

You think of the apple pie back at the bakery. It'd be nice to get a taste of home.

There's just a minute to wolf something down. Time for a quick decision!

IF YOU WAIT TO EAT *DAL BHAT* WITH RUSS, TURN TO PAGE 45.

IF YOU EAT THE APPLE PIE RIGHT NOW, TURN TO PAGE 24.

You thunder up the rocky slope, quickly passing Garrett and Julia, who are already slowing down.

From below, Doc calls, "This climb should take hours—not minutes!" And Julia shouts something about Everest.

But you don't let anything distract you. You keep up the fast pace, and an hour and a half later—

You're first to the top!

But your body is in agony. You're heaving and sweating, and you can't seem to get enough air. You throw up in nearby bushes. *Blech.* After drinking a little water, you manage to get your breathing under control.

An hour later, the others reach the top. They're all laughing together, having enjoyed a slow but steady climb.

You feel Hans's eyes on you. Is he admiring you for your amazing climb? It's hard to tell.

It's not hard to tell how Doc and Russ feel, though. They're shaking their heads.

Russ puts a stern hand on your shoulder. "What did I say about pushing yourself too hard?"

"I know," you say, "and I would have stopped if I felt bad, but I didn't—I just felt all this energy! I'll try to contain it more tomorrow."

Trying to lighten the mood, Julia asks you, "Did you see that view of Everest?"

You shake your head. You were in too much of a hurry.

As you and the team head into Namche Bazaar, the biggest village in the area, you feel a strange kind of clicking in your knee. You must have wrenched it or something when you were cranking up the hill. It doesn't hurt too much, but it's enough to make you wince a little.

Once you're at the lodge where you'll be spending the next two nights, you slowly climb the steps to your room—with your knee feeling just a tiny bit worse with each step.

You think about telling Doc. But then the whole team will figure Hans's doubts about you were right. Maybe, after some rest, your knee will feel better in the morning.

**IF YOU DECIDE TO KEEP YOUR HURT KNEE TO YOURSELF, TURN TO PAGE 39.**

**IF YOU TELL DOC ABOUT YOUR KNEE, TURN TO PAGE 37.**

"Your loss, kid," Jake says. "Guess I'll go on my own."

You watch Jake leave for the icefall and wonder, *Should I have gone with him?*

Five minutes later, the Sherpas arrive at Camp. You jump to your feet, excited to finally meet them. Russ points a Sherpa in his early twenties your way. He gives you a bright smile and a firm handshake.

"My name is Lhakpa, your climbing partner," he says.

"*Namaskar,*" you say, using the formal Nepalese word for hello.

Even though you're sure you botched the pronunciation, Lhakpa's smile broadens. "*Namaste,*" he responds using the more casual greeting. He leads you over to an older Sherpa. "And this is Dorjee Sherpa. He is the sirdar, the head Sherpa."

Dorjee gives you a long look with a furrowed brow and stern eyes and then, after a quick handshake, walks over to Doc to say something. That's not the way you wanted your first meeting with the sirdar to go.

Disappointed, you turn back to Lhakpa. "Did I do something that offended Dorjee?"

Lhakpa pats your shoulder kindly. "You did nothing wrong. Dorjee Sherpa is just worried that you and the two others are too young for this climb."

Before you can say more, the puja ceremony starts. You quickly see why it's important. The Sherpas won't start any climb up Everest until they've received the blessing of the lama, a holy man who has come to Base Camp with them.

During the two hours of the blessing, as incense is burned and prayer flags flap in the breeze, you start to understand that Everest is a sacred mountain. No one here talks about conquering it—there's just respect for this amazing place.

You all reach into a bowl and toss a powder called *tsampa* in the air. Then you smear it all over each others' faces. After the seriousness of the ceremony, it's hysterical. You feel like you're all friends at a party.

Trays of a drink called *chang* are passed around. You, Julia, and Garrett reach for glasses.

"No way," Doc says. "This is alcohol. It's soda for the three of you."

When everyone has a glass, Russ gives a toast. "A good climb is all about using good judgment. Here's to wise choices."

Just as everyone starts dancing in a large circle, Jake returns to Camp.

He looks tired and discouraged. You and Hans break away from the group to talk to him.

"I'm sorry I missed the ceremony," Jake says. "I went to

work on my rappelling technique. The one you taught me, Hans."

Blue eyes flaring, Hans snaps. "Jake, I just showed you that technique *once*. You could have killed yourself."

You go to bed that night feeling very good about your decision not to go with Jake earlier.

Early the next morning, you begin your ascent by entering the treacherous Khumbu Icefall. You leave Base Camp before the sun comes up.

Like all mountainside glaciers, the Khumbu Icefall is a big river of ice that slowly creeps downhill. That might sound peaceful, but it's anything but peaceful in the icefall. Giant towers of ice called seracs can collapse, and deep cracks in the ice called crevasses can open and close without warning.

It's best not to be in the icefall when it's thawing in the hot afternoon sun or when it's refreezing in the evening. These are the most dangerous times, when seracs are more likely to come crashing down on top of you. That's why you're climbing in the early morning.

But really, no time in the icefall is truly safe. *Be careful*, you say to yourself as you climb in the dim light, *be careful* . . .

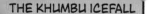
THE KHUMBU ICEFALL

YOUR HARNESS IS CLIPPED TO A "FIXED ROPE" THAT'S CONNECTED TO THE TERRAIN WITH ICE AND SNOW ANCHORS.

THIS DOESN'T LOOK SO SCARY.

WE'LL STAY CLIPPED THROUGH THE ICEFALL. THAT WAY IF YOU FALL INTO A CREVASSE, WE CAN PULL YOU OUT.

BUT I DON'T SEE ANY CREVASSES.

You haven't gone too far along the icy route when Russ says, "Here's a good place for a pit stop. Now's the time to take a pee if you have to. Up ahead, we won't have so much room to spread out."

With that, the others start the tricky process of unclipping from the rope and stepping off the trail to relieve themselves. But you don't have to go, so you wait. A minute or so later, everyone returns. They all clip in again, and you're off.

Five minutes later, you've arrived at the first crevasse. It's like a deep gaping mouth in the icy snow—and pretty terrifying. Because the route is so narrow, there's no way around it. Luckily, the Sherpas have set up a way to go over it. They've turned a regular, everyday ladder into a bridge—and secured each end to the ice on either side of the crevasse.

Doc is the first one to cross the rickety bridge. She moves easily and gracefully, even in heavy boots. You can tell she's a natural athlete and an experienced climber.

Russ turns to you. "Okay, your turn."

And just like that . . . you have to pee. *Really* bad.

**IF YOU UNCLIP, TAKE OFF THE HARNESS, AND WALK OFF THE ROUTE A WAYS TO RELIEVE YOURSELF, TURN TO PAGE 106.**

**IF YOU JUST STAY CLIPPED AND PEE NEAR THE OTHER CLIMBERS, TURN TO PAGE 60.**

You knock on Doc and Russ's door down the hall. When they answer, you tell them about your injured knee.

As they walk you back to your room, Doc says, "Why didn't you tell us before?"

Russ shakes his head. "You probably didn't want us to say 'told you so' for going too fast up Namche Hill, right? You're smart to tell us now, though, so we can deal with this."

Doc examines your leg. "You'll be fine," she says, "but you'll need to rest for at least a day. Ice that knee and keep it elevated. No walking around the village for you."

"Too bad," Russ says. "That means you'll miss having lunch with us tomorrow. I know a place here that serves the best *dal bhat*!"

*Dal bhat*? Doc explains that it's rice and lentils and usually a green vegetable.

*Hmm.* Missing that doesn't sound like such a bad deal. You'll stick with the granola bars in your backpack for now.

The morning after your rest day, you're going stir-crazy in your room. From your window, you can see—and smell—a small bakery down the road. *Ah*, apple pie. Smells like home.

That afternoon, Doc gives you the green light for a short walk around Namche Bazaar. "It'll be good for your knee," she says, "and it'll help get your body used to the higher altitude."

You find Garrett and Julia, and the three of you explore the village. It's way busier than you thought it'd be. There are tons of little shops selling T-shirts and climbing gear. But the places that really catch your eye—and your nose?

The bakeries.

You find yourself standing in front of one, drooling as you stare through the window at the apple pies and pastries. Trekkers like you go in and out of the bakery. But the locals just walk by.

"Come on," Garrett says to you. "You've got to try that *dal bhat* Russ loves."

*Really?* you think, remembering Doc's description of the dish.

"The place Russ likes is up there," Julia points at a teahouse in the distance.

But the apple pie is right here. And the most important thing is for you to eat a lot to keep your energy up, right?

---

**IF YOU GRAB A QUICK SLICE OF APPLE PIE, GO TO PAGE 24.**

**IF YOU DECIDE TO WAIT AND TRY *DAL BHAT*, GO TO PAGE 50.**

The next morning, the ache in your knee has doubled. It takes all your concentration to hide your limp.

*I can do this,* you think as you struggle to walk normally.

You're heading up a slope when you feel something tear—in your *good* leg this time.

"*Ahh*!" You fall to the ground. By favoring your bad knee, you've hurt yourself even worse!

Doc rushes to you. "What is it? What happened?"

Groaning, you tell her about injuring your knee.

"I'm sorry," she says, examining you. "The knee might've healed, but now you've torn a ligament in your other leg. You're going home."

She's right. You can barely stand—let alone climb Everest.

But how will you get to Lukla airport? There are no cars. Doc points to a passing yak.

"It's a yak ambulance for you," she says.

A two-day ride on that smelly, hairy beast? Talk about adding insult—not to mention yak breath!—to injury.

THE END

"Whoa," you breathe.

"Are you okay?" Doc shouts. "Answer me!"

You wave. "I'm okay," you call. "It's a good thing I just took that pee break. Otherwise, I'd need an extra pair of pants."

You're still in the middle of the ladder, right where it droops down a little. You think about crawling the rest of the way to the other side. But you're even more determined now to walk.

You step onto the solid snow and Garrett gives you another high five. "Way to go, mate. You had us a bit worried."

"Like to keep people on their crampons," you say with a chuckle. After Hans crosses the ladder, you shake his hand. "Thanks for the advice. You were right: I needed to lean for a tight line."

Something softens in the Swiss climber's blue eyes, but just slightly. Then he says with a shrug, "It's my job to help out."

After the team crosses a few more crevasses, Russ says, "Okay, we've gone high enough for today. Let's head back to Base Camp."

$\longrightarrow$

The next day, you climb all the way through the icefall and arrive in Camp One. But the visit is short, and the following afternoon you're back in Base Camp, where the air has more oxygen.

A four-day rest and then it's time to go back through the icefall. Again.

By the time you reach Camp One on the seventh day after your first ascent, it's safe to say you're pretty sick of the Khumbu Icefall. Luckily, the plan is to overnight in Camp One and keep going to Camp Two in the morning. As sirdar, Dorjee has led the rest of the Sherpas ahead to set it up.

That night, you're hanging out in Camp One with Julia and Garrett, drinking tea, when Julia coughs. "I'm fine," she says when you ask if she's okay. "Tea must have gone down the wrong way, that's all." She grins. "Can you believe we don't have to go back to Base Camp tomorrow?"

"I know," you say. "It's awesome."

But things really aren't awesome, are they? In fact, your head feels like it's in a vise. And the pain isn't new. Each time you've arrived in Camp One, you haven't felt great, and you always figured you'd feel better on your next trip up. You're still not feeling better, though. You took the aspirin Doc gave you for the headache, but it's not working.

The next morning, things are worse. As you and the team are getting set to climb, Garrett asks, "You want some grub? Protein bar?"

You shake your head. The thought of food makes you queasy.

"You're not hungry? How about thirsty?" Julia asks, sounding a little alarmed. "You might have altitude sickness."

"No way," you say in a whisper, not wanting the others to overhear your conversation. You couldn't bear to be sent back to Base Camp so soon. The icefall again? Right now? No way.

"We've been in Nepal for over a month now. My body should be fine at this altitude," you say.

Doc is walking by and hears your whispering. "Something wrong?"

"Nothing," you say, trying to smile. "We're all fine."

She hesitates for a second. "If one of you isn't up for the climb right now, I can hang out with you here for a bit."

You repeat that all's well, and Doc finally leaves the three of you alone again.

"Maybe it's just the heat," Garrett says. "It's blazing."

"Sure," you say, "I guess that could be it."

Then Russ calls over to you: "We're pressing on to Camp Two. Let's go!"

**IF YOU DECIDE TO WAIT WITH DOC AT CAMP ONE UNTIL YOU FEEL BETTER, TURN TO PAGE 65.**

**IF YOU CLIMB ON WITH THE OTHERS RIGHT NOW, TURN TO PAGE 69.**

Having chosen not to use a rope to connect you with Doc, you start your climb. Doc is right behind you.

After a few hours of walking up a gentle slope, you start to feel at ease. Compared to all those scary climbs through the Khumbu Icefall, this is a piece of cake!

Then you come upon a short snow bridge across a crevasse. The bridge is about as wide as a sidewalk back home, and it appears to be well supported by a thick base.

*This looks a lot more solid than those bridges we were crossing in the icefall*, you think. *No problem.*

But right as you get to the middle—

*Whomp!*

The bridge collapses, and you fall . . . and fall . . . until you land on a jumble of ice blocks with a loud *crack*!

"Are you okay?" Doc shouts down to you urgently.

You look at your right leg, which is bending in a way that no leg should ever bend, and your heart sinks as you say, "*No.*"

Your climb is over.

THE END

You make it to the team lunch on time—and totally get why *dal bhat's* a big hit here in Nepal. It's delicious!

As you gulp down a second helping, you feel your energy level cranking back up. During the rest of the day in Namche Bazaar, you feel yourself getting stronger.

The following morning, your team heads out for its next stop on the route to Base Camp—Tengboche. The small village is home to a famous monastery.

"Whoa," you say when you see the majestic buildings that make up the monastery. As you step inside the shadowy prayer hall, you smell the sweet smoke of incense. Your eyes run over the vibrant paintings of Buddhist symbols and gods.

You're greeted by the Rimpoche, a spiritual leader, an old man wearing maroon and gold robes. As you all gather around, he starts speaking in Tibetan.

"Is he giving us directions to Everest?" Jake jokes.

Russ shushes him. "It's a blessing. He's wishing us a safe journey and telling us to be respectful of the mountain."

The Rimpoche hands each of you a red string called a *sungdhi*. Russ explains that you're supposed to tie it around your neck, to carry the blessing with you. As Julia ties yours, you silently promise to honor the words of the Rimpoche. As you turn to go, he smiles at you as if he heard your thoughts.

After four more days of hiking through villages, you arrive at Base Camp, a giant mass of tents from all the expeditions that will be heading to the summit this season. From here, you'll make lots of trips to the higher camps to help your body get used to the ever-thinning air.

When you get to your team's area, you see a bunch of blue tents, including a sleeping tent for each person, and a big dining tent for everyone to eat and hang out in. There's even a laptop with an Internet connection in the dining tent.

"Who set up our camp?" Julia asks.

"The Sherpas we hired for our expedition," Russ explains.

Each climber, including you, will be assigned his or her own Sherpa. Because they live in such high altitudes, Sherpas are amazing climbers.

"We'll finally get to meet them!" you say.

"Sorry," Russ says. "The Sherpas went back down for more equipment. They'll be back in a few days for our first climb."

You spend part of the next two days helping Doc test the equipment at Base Camp. Oxygen bottles, goggles, radios, crampons (the spikes you attach to your boots for traction on ice)—all have to be in working order. As you work, you slather on sunblock, surprised by how warm and sunny it is.

There's time for fun at Base Camp, too. Garrett brought a soccer ball, and you strike up a match with a nearby camp of German climbers. It's a blast, even though the "field" is just a small patch of rock-covered ice. Garrett even comes up with a good name for the match: Top of the World Cup.

After four days at Base Camp, it's almost time to make your first ascent. The morning before your climb, you stop by Garrett's tent to see if he wants to go for a walk, but he's feeling queasy, probably because of the altitude. You're about to head off by yourself when Jake steps out of his tent.

"Hey there, kiddo," Jake says, wandering over to you. "Hope you're not too tuckered out after all that soccer. You have a lot of tricky climbing ahead of you."

"I've got it covered," you say. You know Jake is paying a lot for this trip, so you want him to think you're worth it.

Jake laughs. "You remind me of myself when I was your age. Always knew what was best."

He points to three stacks of rocks on a hill in the distance. "See those chortens? They're memorials to climbers who died here. Some died right over there, in avalanches in the Khumbu Icefall. It's a treacherous place. You ready for it tomorrow?"

"Sure," you say, but *avalanches* is echoing in your head.

Jake must hear doubt in your voice. "Sounds like you could use a confidence booster. I know a special ascending technique that will get you through the icefall safely. Let's head up to the edge of the icefall now, and I'll show it to you."

"What about the puja ceremony?" you ask.

Russ told you about the puja ceremony yesterday. You're not sure what it'll be like—you just know that it's some kind of blessing before the climb, and you're waiting for the Sherpas to arrive so it can begin.

Jake shrugs. "There's no other time to do this. I think your safety is a lot more important than some little ceremony."

What do you say?

IF YOU SKIP THE PUJA CEREMONY TO GO WITH JAKE, TURN TO PAGE 55.

IF YOU TELL JAKE YOU'D RATHER STAY FOR THE CEREMONY, TURN TO PAGE 31.

Russ is totally right: the *dal bhat* at this teahouse *is* awesome.

In fact, when Doc says the team will wait an extra day before heading to Base Camp, to give your knee time to rest—you're kind of glad. You'll get to chow down on more *dal bhat*, all the while getting stronger.

Then it's time to say good-bye to Namche Bazaar. The next few days, you take it slowly as you hike higher into the mountains. When you reach Base Camp on the tenth day of your trek, you're surprised. It's huge! It's a whole village of tents swarming with people from different expeditions. Your team's area has been set up by Sherpas—locals hired by Russ and Doc to handle the logistics of your expedition. In fact, Russ is leading two Sherpas over to you now.

"This is Lhakpa Sherpa," Russ says, introducing you to the younger of the two. "He'll be watching out for you and climbing with you on the day we summit."

Lhakpa gives you a smile and a solid handshake. You like him right away. You're glad he's the Sherpa you'll be teaming up with.

"And this is Dorjee Sherpa," Russ continues. "He's an old friend of mine and our expedition's sirdar."

Dorjee's smile and handshake are not nearly as friendly. It's clear that Dorjee is not happy with how young you are. *Great*, you think, *someone else who has doubts about me!*

A week later, you leave Base Camp for Camp One. Too bad the only way to reach it is through the Khumbu Icefall.

The icefall is home to deadly avalanches, giant ice towers—called seracs—that collapse without warning, and shifting crevasses that have to be crossed on ladder bridges. The day before, Russ helped you practice your climbing skills here, so you think you're up to the challenge.

When you reach the bottom of the icefall, Garrett is looking kind of green. You ask if he's okay. He just nods.

"Time to gear up, team," Russ says. "Let's get those crampons on."

Crampons are the spikes that attach to the bottoms of your boots. They'll give you traction on the ice. But when you try to put on your crampons, you discover they don't fit. They fit yesterday!

"Yesterday you put them on in the heat of the day," Russ says. "Now it's in the early morning, and everything's frozen, so they've contracted a bit."

Russ takes out his multi-tool to adjust the screws on your crampons.

"We'll catch up," Russ tells Doc.

"Okay," she says, and she

heads off, leading Julia, Hans, and Jake up into the icefall. Garrett says he'll wait with you.

"I need a rest anyway," he says.

It takes a couple of minutes, but the adjustment works. Your crampons fit. By now, though, Garrett looks even greener.

"You all right?" Russ asks him.

"My belly aches, and I'm feeling a bit dizzy," he says. "Sorry, mate, but I think I need to go back to Base Camp."

Russ nods, and then looks at you. "You could catch up with the others. Or you could go back down with us now and climb again tomorrow."

It is getting late in the morning, and the sun is hot. But it sure would be great to finally get to Camp One after a whole week at Base Camp. You guess it would only take about twenty minutes to catch up to the others, and you'd be clipped to a fixed rope the whole time. Should you go for it?

**IF YOU KEEP CLIMBING, TURN TO PAGE 82.**

**IF YOU GO BACK DOWN, TURN TO PAGE 67.**

"All right!" Jake sounds like an excited little kid. "We'll get this technique down and wow the rest of the team when we climb through the icefall again tomorrow."

You can see why Jake is good at making video games—he loves winning.

"Just half an hour more," you say. "That should be enough time to rappel down this serac at least two more times."

"Great!" Jake nods. "But we should bump up the difficulty and set up in a different spot."

He points to an even bigger serac that's a short climb away. By the time you get up there and set up the ropes, you're really sweating from the heat, and twenty minutes has passed.

"Let's rappel down at the same time," Jake says. "We can each rappel off one ice screw. Then maybe we'll have time to do it again."

It'd be safer to go down one at a time, securing your rope to *both* ice screws, as you've been doing all day. But you're tired of arguing with Jake. You'll get back to Base Camp faster if you go along with what he wants now.

"All right, Jake," you say. "Let's do it."

Without telling anyone where you're going, you and Jake grab your gear and head out of Base Camp.

"You'll be glad you came along," Jake says to you, patting you on the back.

But when you get your first look at the Khumbu Icefall, you're not so sure. There are scary places in the world, and this has to be in the top three. This sliding glacier is a twisted terrain filled with ice towers—called seracs—that can collapse when they start to melt in the afternoon heat or refreeze in the evening. Then there are the deep, seemingly bottomless crevasses that can open and close like hungry mouths that are just hoping to swallow a couple of climbers.

You know Russ and Doc wouldn't like you and Jake being up here on your own. But you're here now, so you might as well get some climbing practice in.

"Okay, Jake," you say. "What's the special rappelling technique you want to show me?"

Jake grins, excited to be in charge. "It's a special kind of hitch. I don't remember the name, but I'll just show you."

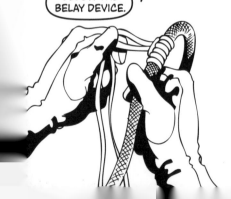

YOU PULL JAKE BACK FROM THE EDGE, AND HE FALLS AT YOUR FEET.

"Jake," you say, "that prussik wouldn't have worked as a backup brake because you didn't clip it to anything. You should have clipped it to your leg loop."

Jake looks embarrassed. "Oops," he says.

It's clear now that it was a mistake sneaking out here. A big one. But, as you told yourself before, you *are* here now, so you might as well make the best of it.

Once you've set up your gear correctly, you and Jake practice rappelling down the ice tower. As you climb back up the ice tower after your second rappel, the midday sun is pounding down on you.

"This should be our last rappel," you say. "I'm beat, and the others will be wondering where we are."

Jake gives you a look of genuine gratitude. "You really helped me today. I won't forget it. I have one more favor to ask. Let's just stay another half hour and keep working on the technique."

**IF YOU SAY . . .**

**"NO, REALLY, JUST ONE MORE RAPPEL," TURN TO PAGE 21.**

**"OKAY, A HALF HOUR MORE," TURN TO PAGE 53.**

Unclipped from the fixed rope, you follow Hans off the path. It's just a short distance to a pile of giant ice blocks that must have formed during an avalanche. The mound is four times as tall as you are.

Hans points to the top and says, "Up there you'll have the best angle for your photo."

You scramble up the pile and find that Hans is right. The view is amazing. From here, you can see down a big stretch of the valley. You take out your camera—

That's not the sound of your camera. It's a block of ice breaking. Right under your feet. You tumble sideways, fall, and hit the ground hard, feeling your forearm crack.

Your arm is broken. Even as Hans rushes to your side, you know your climb up Everest is finished.

Not exactly the picture-perfect ending you'd been hoping for, is it?

**THE END**

"I need some space here, guys!" you shout. Everyone takes a very small step away, or at least turns his or her head.

You have to go so bad, there's no time to be embarrassed. You just go.

"Thanks, everyone," you say, once you're all buttoned up again. "I *really* needed that."

Garrett gives you a gloved high five. "Just remind me not to eat the snow when you're around."

"Okay, let's get moving!" Russ calls to you from across the crevasse. "We don't want to be out here too long under the sun."

You stand on the edge again and look down—from this angle you can't see the bottom.

"For this first crevasse at least, I want you three to crawl across the ladder," Russ says, pointing to you, Garrett, and Julia. "Got it?"

You nod and get on your hands and knees. You start to crawl very slowly across the ladder. The view is pretty terrifying: straight down into nothingness.

It's beyond freaky, and you look back in a panic. You lock stares with Hans. His hard blue eyes seem to say, *I knew it. This kid can't handle it.*

That's all the motivation you need. You start crawling again. Soon you have a rhythm as you go from rung to rung.

You get across and climb to your feet.

"Welcome to the other side," Russ says. You duck before he can put you in a headlock.

Once you're all across, it's time to move on to the next crevasse. Russ crosses first to test out the ladder bridge. "I think you three can take this one walking upright," he says.

Garrett goes first. He's shaking a little but makes it to the other side pretty fast. Then it's your turn.

"Any advice?" you shout over to Garrett.

"Sure," the Aussie says. "Don't fall!"

"Ha-ha," you say and get started. With a clang, your crampon hits the first rung. You make sure it's secure. You put your other foot down in front of you on the next rung.

And before you know it, you're in the middle of the ladder. Halfway there. You pause for just a second to catch your breath, and then . . .

*Lean forward? Is Hans nuts?*

If you do that, you could topple right over!

You're secured to the fixed line, so if you fall off the ladder, the rope will catch you before you hit the bottom of the crevasse—but do you really want to test it?

You've got to make a choice, and fast!

**IF YOU LISTEN TO HANS AND LEAN FORWARD, GO TO PAGE 40.**

**IF YOU IGNORE HANS, GO TO PAGE 71.**

It's tough to wave good-bye to the rest of the team.

"I'm never going to catch back up," you mumble.

"Remember, we're here for a long time. This is a marathon, not a sprint," Doc says. Then she adds, "In surfing, sometimes you have to wait a long time for the right wave. That same is true up here. You've got to wait until you feel right to make the climb."

The pep talk actually makes you feel a little better. You and Doc duck inside a tent to get out of the searing sun. As you lay down, you feel really drowsy, and soon you're asleep.

When you wake up a few hours later, Doc starts asking questions. "Are you disoriented? Dizzy? Thirsty?"

You answer "no" until her last question: "Hungry?"

"Thought you'd never ask," you say. You're starving!

"That's a great sign," she says.

You're anxious to get going. "Come on, Doc, can I climb tomorrow or not?" you ask, hoping Doc won't hold you up.

"I know I seem like a stick-in-the-mud," she says. "But, believe it or not, I remember what it was like to climb at your age and how I wanted to be treated. I remember I wanted guidance, but also the freedom to make choices."

She thinks for a second, and then pats your arm. "You're ready. Tomorrow we'll catch up with the others."

Morning brings a small layer of fresh snow up to your ankles. You're feeling stronger, and you're glad you waited.

To reach Camp Two, you'll cross the Western Cwm, also known as the Valley of Silence. Doc explains that *Cwm* is a Welsh word that sounds like *coom*. It's a sloping valley that should be a piece of cake compared to the icefall.

There are no fixed ropes to guide you most of the way. You know that sometimes fresh snow can hide crevasses, but Doc seems confident you'll be able to find a safe path by following the footprints the team made the day before.

"If that worries you," Doc says, "we can rope up together so we're safe when there are no fixed lines . . ." She trails off, as if recalling what she said yesterday. "You know, I want you to make your own choice. What do you want to do?"

IF YOU ASK DOC TO ROPE UP WITH YOU, TURN TO PAGE 77.

IF YOU CLIMB WITHOUT A ROPE, TURN TO PAGE 44.

You head back to Base Camp and get a good night's rest. The next morning, you awaken to this sound:

*Wham! Wham!*

Something is slamming into your tent. You unzip the flap. It's still dark outside, but you can see Garrett's grinning face as he gets set to throw another snowball at your tent.

"Rise and shine!" he chimes, clearly feeling better than yesterday. "Russ wanted me to get you up so the three of us can get climbing. We'll meet up with the rest of the team at Camp One."

"Glad to see you're back to your old self," you say. Then eyeing the snowball in his hand, you add with a laugh, "Well, kind of glad."

In the darkness, you and Garrett follow Russ out of camp and to the Khumbu Icefall. Russ explains it's safer to climb early in the day. Later in the day, when it gets warmer, there can be more avalanches and ice collapses.

"Just like we practiced," Russ says when you reach the first crevasse with a ladder bridge, "I want you two to go across on your hands and knees."

You and Garrett crawl across the ladder with no trouble, and Russ lets you cross the second crevasse standing up.

But when you reach the next ladder, Russ discovers that it has shifted slightly.

"Looks secure," Russ says. "But I'll go over to the other side and make sure."

To get there, he descends into the crevasse until he reaches a point where he can cross over to the other side and then climb back up.

As you and Garrett wait, the sun continues to rise. It reflects off the slick ice around you, and soon it's unbearably hot. There's a sound like a tree falling in the distance—and you know an ice tower must have toppled over.

Red and sweaty, Garrett walks over to a nearby shady spot next to a giant serac.

"Oh, yes!" he shouts. "It's much cooler in the shade." He waves for you to join him. "We can wait here until Russ is ready for us to cross."

You look at Garrett standing in the shade. It *does* look cooler next to the serac.

**IF YOU STAND IN THE SHADE WITH GARRETT, TURN TO PAGE 22.**

**IF YOU STAY OUT IN THE SUN, TURN TO PAGE 74.**

The climb to Camp Two is a struggle. Your headache is way worse. Each step you take feels like a soccer player is kicking you in the back of the skull—with really sharp cleats.

Just as Camp Two comes into view in the distance, you slip on the ice. *Wham!* Doc doesn't see it, but Garrett does.

He grabs your arm. "You need to say something if you're not up for this."

As you shake free, you say, "I'm fine." Actually, it's more of a snarl. Suddenly, you don't want to be touched.

Besides, you're so close to Camp Two—just a few hundred more painful, agonizing steps.

And guess what? You make it. You showed everyone! You see all the tents the Sherpas have set up . . . but where's the one with the giant heat lamp?

"Hey," you say, "where's that big warm thing?"

"What?" Julia asks.

Confusion and pain fill your head. Then you pass out.

When you wake up, you're in a tent with an oxygen mask. Doc explains that you have HACE—high-altitude cerebral edema. Your brain is swelling, and they need to get you down the mountain and to a hospital. Now.

Your climb is over.

THE END

That night, you and the team leave Camp Four, heading for the summit—finally!

"Keep your focus!" Lhakpa tells you. He's climbing behind you, toward the back of the line, and he's just noticed you slip.

You've only been climbing up the steep, icy slope for about an hour. But you're already exhausted, and you haven't been placing your crampons on the ice as carefully as you should. It's just too hard. So you've been pulling more and more on the fixed line.

At one point, all of your weight is on the line, and before you know it, you're sliding downhill. You squeeze the rope tighter, but your frostbitten fingers don't seem to be working.

Then you fall backward—

*Smack!*

—you ram into Lhakpa. You tumble together. By the time you stop rolling, you've broken your collar bone, and Lhakpa is clutching his broken ankle.

It's back to Base Camp for both of you. The summit's no longer an option.

And who's to blame? You can only point a finger—one with painful frostbite—at yourself.

**THE END**

*Great*, you think to yourself as you dangle in the crevasse. *If only I had just leaned forward!*

The rope would have tightened and helped stop your wobbling. Instead, you're in this mess.

And it keeps getting worse, because now you're tangled in the two fixed ropes.

"Hang in there!" Russ shouts. "I'll drop you a rope and pull you out."

*Another rope!* Just what you need.

You twist your body so you can look at the tangled ropes. You spot a solution—you could unclip from one rope, hang from the other one, sort out the tangle, and climb up yourself. It sure would be great to emerge from this mess fast, without needing a rescue.

**IF YOU SORT OUT THE TANGLE YOURSELF, TURN TO PAGE 83.**

**IF YOU WAIT FOR THE ROPE FROM RUSS, TURN TO PAGE 95.**

You push the fogged goggles up onto your forehead. You have to squint against the bright light of the sun bouncing off the snow, but—

*Yes! Now I can see!*

You kick your right foot into the ice. Instantly, your body starts to stabilize, and you're no longer about to fall. Pulling on the rope, you begin kick stepping your way up the rest of the ice bulge.

"Put those goggles back on!" Doc shouts.

But you don't want to stop. You're so close to the top of the bulge. Just a few more steps!

Doc rushes over to you and pushes the goggles down over your eyes.

"What's the big deal?" you ask. "They were only off for about two minutes, and my eyes feel fine."

"Don't you get it?" Doc demands. "That light might have burned your corneas, and you won't even know it yet. Signs of snow blindness might not show up for hours."

And she's right. It's not until the next morning at Camp Three that you realize you should have listened to her.

You're in your tent, just waking up, and suddenly it's like a dial in each eyeball has been turned to MASSIVE PAIN. Your eyes are on fire. Tears stream down your face, and you can't even open your eyelids. You start rubbing your eyes, calling out for help.

Russ is the first one to arrive. "Stop rubbing them!" he tells you. "You're just making things worse."

Doc is next. She pries your lids open so she can take a look. "You've got a bad case of snow blindness," she says. "We have to get you down to Base Camp and then on to the hospital."

"No," you insist. "I just need to rest."

But the two hot pokers in your eyes say otherwise. And it will be hard for you to climb to the summit if your eyes won't work!

It takes the help of the entire team to get you back down to Base Camp. The going is very slow. By the time you all reach camp, you're exhausted.

As you say good-bye to the team before heading off to the hospital, you feel the tears flowing again.

But this time, it's for a different reason.

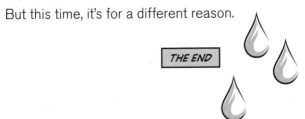

THE END

Looking at the serac next to Garrett, you suddenly remember what Russ said about the sun's heat causing avalanches— and serac collapses.

"Get away from there, Garrett!" you shout. "Now!"

And it's a good thing he listens to you. Just as he steps out of the shade, the serac cracks and the top plunges right on the spot where he'd been standing.

"That was way too close!" Garrett rushes over to you. "Thanks! Looks like you might just have saved my neck!"

Four hours later, you climb out of the icefall and finally reach Camp One. The rest of the expedition is waiting for you. You're all together again, including Lhakpa, Dorjee, and the other Sherpas who have set up camp. This is your first night as a group at such a high altitude.

You decide to celebrate with a big team dinner. Russ has a surprise, too.

"I'd yell at anyone else for wasting energy and lugging stuff like this up the mountain," he says with a grin. "But I thought we could use a treat."

He pulls out two plastic bottles of grape and lemon syrup, explaining you can squirt the syrup on snow to make your own snow cone. There's something hilarious about eating an icy treat on the side of a giant icy mountain.

"Just remember, dinner before dessert," Doc says. Then, realizing how parental she sounds, she laughs. "Wow, I can't believe I said that!"

Soon, dinner is ready, and you pick up your plate of *dal bhat* and grilled meat. Looking around, you notice that Hans, Julia, and Garrett are eating by themselves, standing in a loose cluster around the camp stove. You could stand next to any of them and strike up a conversation. Where do you eat?

**IF YOU EAT WITH...**

**GARRETT, TO FIND OUT MORE ABOUT HIM, TURN TO PAGE 107.**

**JULIA, TO GET TO KNOW HER BETTER, TURN TO PAGE 98.**

**HANS, TO HEAR HIS STORY, TURN TO PAGE 103.**

Even though you're clipped onto the rope, you grab it with both hands. You brace yourself as the three-story wall of ice and snow plummets toward you.

Suddenly, you're having serious doubts about this plan. But it's too late. "Wait!" you shout, as if the avalanche can hear you. Then—

*Blam!*

The wall hammers into you with monumental force. Your body turns over and over like you're a wet sock inside a clothes dryer. Snow, ice, arms, legs—all pass before your eyes, and you close them tight. The sound is deafening.

Then it's still. Very still. The avalanche is over.

You try moving. You can't. Opening your eyes, you see only darkness, and you know you're buried deep in the ice and snow. You try yelling, but you doubt anyone can hear you.

As you slowly run out of air, your brain plays tricks on you. You start to imagine a giant yellow excavator rolling up the icefall to dig you out. It's a happy thought.

*It's almost here,* you think to yourself. *Almost here. . . .*

**THE END**

"Good plan," Doc says. She hands you a climbing rope, and you tie it to your harness while Doc does the same. In a few minutes, you and Doc are "roped up" together and ready to climb toward Camp Two.

The mountains on either side block the wind from entering the valley. It's very, very quiet with only the sound of your breathing and the crunching of your crampons.

You whisper like you're in the library, "Gee, I wonder how they came up with the name Valley of Silence?"

*CRACK!* You jump as dual avalanches thunder down on either side of you. The valley is wide, and there isn't any danger. Still, it's pretty dramatic.

"Maybe the valley doesn't like sarcasm," Doc calls back to you from the lead position.

"Too bad," you reply, "because I was just going to say maybe it should be renamed the Furnace of Everest."

It's true—even though you'd expect to be cold up here in the mountains, surrounded by snow and ice, the valley is incredibly hot under the scorching sun. The heat is getting to you, and you stumble but manage to keep from falling.

"How're you doing?" Doc asks, the worry already creeping back into her voice.

You're about to answer—when you look up and stop in your tracks.

"*Wow*," is all you can say.

Doc turns to follow your gaze. "*Wow*," she says too.

From this spot, you can see something that you haven't seen since arriving at Base Camp—the top of Mount Everest. For weeks, it's been blocked from view. But now there it is. The summit. Your goal. You feel renewed determination flood through you, and you power on through the valley.

Two hours later, you enter Camp Two for the first time. And it's like a long-lost hero has arrived. The team rushes to greet you. Julia and Garrett both put their arms around you and walk with you into camp. The Sherpas are here, too, and Dorjee gives you a nod—still not very friendly, but warmer.

The only one who doesn't even acknowledge you is Hans—you spot him melting snow over the camp stove.

Russ hands you a cup of the melted snow, and you gulp it down. You've had a total of eight hours of climbing today, and you're exhausted. You have to get some shut-eye. Now.

Early the next morning, you wake up to the sound of Julia coughing in the next tent over. It goes on and on. There's no snooze button for that kind of alarm. But you wish there were. It's only 6:00 a.m., and you're still wiped out from yesterday.

Though you know you should be, you're not very hungry. As you gnaw on a protein bar for breakfast, Russ mentions, "Today is all about getting your body used to this altitude. You can speed things up by taking a walk around camp."

Two hours later, you're beat and already thinking about a nap. That's when you spot Lhakpa heading toward the edge of camp. Joining the Sherpa on a walk could be your chance to acclimatize and also talk with him one-on-one. Then again, you don't think you've ever been so tired—and a nap is sounding better and better.

**IF YOU GO FOR A WALK WITH LHAKPA, TURN TO PAGE 89.**

**IF YOU TAKE A QUICK NAP, TURN TO PAGE 133.**

You fumble with the clip,
but you're panicking and
your hands slip—
*Hurry! Hurry!*
You unclip from the fixed
rope and race for the serac, diving
behind it and using it as a shield.
Just then the avalanche strikes.

With the force of a tsunami, the snow and ice wallop into the serac. The serac protects you—at least for the most part. When the avalanche ends, you're coated with shards of ice and snow.

You stand up just as Doc and Hans reach you. You're shaken but okay. As you continue your climb to Camp One, you think, *I'm the luckiest person alive!*

Six days later, you climb through the icefall again and reach Camp One for the second time.

Sorry to say, the headache you felt the first time you arrived at Camp One is back with a vengeance. The next morning, your head's still pounding, and you have no appetite.

As everyone preps to climb on to Camp Two, Russ asks you, "Is something wrong?"

Doc adds, "If you need rest, I'll wait here with you until you feel better, and then we'll catch up with the others."

You want to stay with the team and prove you're strong enough for the climb. But your aching body might be telling you something.

**IF YOU TELL DOC YOU'RE NOT FEELING WELL, TURN TO PAGE 130.**

**IF YOU SAY YOU'RE FINE AND CLIMB ON, TURN TO PAGE 69.**

"Be careful!" Russ tells you as he starts the descent with Garrett.

"Absolutely," you say and climb on along the fixed rope—but not too fast.

*I'll be fine,* you tell yourself as you pass in the shadow of a giant five-story serac. Doc, Julia, Hans, and Jake are just up ahead.

"Hello!" you shout to them. But a rumbling noise—like a train heading your way—drowns out your voice.

Julia looks at you and then up the mountain. She shouts something over and over. You can't hear her, but you can guess what she's saying:

*Avalanche!*

You turn to see a tidal wave of snow rocketing straight toward you. You have just seconds until it strikes.

The huge serac might shelter you. But you'd have to unclip from the fixed rope to get there.

**IF YOU STAY CLIPPED TO THE FIXED ROPE, TURN TO PAGE 76.**

**IF YOU UNCLIP TO TAKE SHELTER BEHIND THE SERAC, TURN TO PAGE 80.**

You unclip from one of the fixed ropes. Now all your weight is on the other rope, and you start to fall.

And fall.

*Come on*, you say to the rope, as if it can understand you. *Catch me!*

The rope must have gathered a lot of slack up on the ladder, you realize in horror, because it never goes tight.

And then you smash into the side of the crevasse.

*Crack!*

That's the sound of your leg breaking, and maybe a couple of ribs.

As you lay moaning, Russ and Doc rappel down to you. They help you back to the top of the crevasse. You're alive, but you're too beat up to continue the climb.

"We'll have to evacuate you by helicopter from Base Camp," Doc tells you.

It's over for you—no record for being part of the youngest team to summit Everest.

Your busted ribs make it hard to talk.

And your busted pride makes it even harder to overhear Hans saying to Jake, "I saw this coming."

**THE END**

"You did *what*?" Doc demands when you tell her about busting up your knee on your trip with Jake to the icefall. She's red-in-the-face mad—and so's Russ.

Doc examines your leg. "This knee should be fine. Probably just needs a day of rest, ice, and elevation."

"Glad to hear it," Russ says. "Now I'm going to have a little chat with Jake."

→

Two days later, your knee's feeling better, and you join the rest of the team in the icefall on your way to Camp One. To get across the crevasses you can't go around, you'll cross ladders that have been laid flat to form bridges.

"Normally, I'd say crawl across the first bridge to get used to it," Russ calls to you from the other side, after he crosses. "But your knee is probably too sore for that. So you're going to have to walk. You up for it?"

It's pretty terrifying, but you nod. "No problem!"

This must be how a fly feels stuck in a spider's web.

You're trapped, tangled in the ropes, and dangling over a dangerous drop that just might kill you.

"Hold on!" Russ calls to you. "I'm going to toss you a rope to pull you out!"

*Another rope?*

You're already caught up in the two fixed lines. How will another rope help you?

"We'll get you out of there in a minute!" Doc shouts.

You feel panic growing in your belly. A minute sounds like forever. If you just unclip from one of the fixed lines, you think you could free yourself from the jumble of ropes and climb out on your own much faster.

"Don't move!" Russ says.

Easy for him to say. He's not stuck here. You could wait for a new rope, or you could unclip very fast and be out of this tangle in the blink of an eye.

**IF YOU UNCLIP FROM THE FIXED ROPE TO GET UNTANGLED, TURN TO PAGE 83.**

**IF YOU WAIT FOR RUSS TO TOSS YOU A ROPE AND PULL YOU OUT, TURN TO PAGE 95.**

"Lhakpa!" you call, running over to him. By the time you catch up, you're sucking air.

"Can—I—" you gasp. You're too out of breath to say: *Can I come along with you?*

Luckily, Lhakpa seems to get it.

"Sure," he says with a warm smile. "I was going to ask you to come with me anyway, but you seemed to need a rest."

"I'm all right," you say. "Or I *will* be once I get more used to the altitude."

He nods. "A short hike will help."

As you walk, you ask Lhakpa how he picked up such fluent English. He explains that he's been around English-speaking climbers for years, first as a cook at Base Camp, and then as a climbing Sherpa.

Ten minutes later, the two of you stop to take in the view. You look around. The scenery is stunning. From Mount Lhotse to Everest itself, there are tons of things to see. But then Lhakpa points to the ice under his feet.

"This spot is where my last climb ended," he says. "I was helping to bring down a climber who had altitude sickness. He panicked, and we both fell. I broke my wrist. That finished my climb, short of my goal. Again."

"Wait," you say. "You've never been to the top?"

Lhakpa shakes his head. "You and I have the same dream. To climb Everest. I am the youngest of five children. We are farmers. When I said I wanted to climb, my family thought I'd be happy as a cook at Base Camp. But how can you look at the majesty of Everest and not want to go to the top?"

You nod in agreement.

"Together, we can both reach our dream," Lhakpa says, with another warm smile. "Now let's head back to camp so you can rest."

After the team takes another trip down to Base Camp, you're back at Camp Two three days later. It's four in the morning when Garrett sticks his head in your tent and says, "Ready to face the face?"

"Do we have a choice?" you ask, knowing the answer is no.

The western side of Lhotse is called the Lhotse Face. It rises about three times the height of the Empire State Building. The steep wall of blue ice is the only way to get to Camp Three.

As you're leaving camp, Russ tosses you a bandanna to wear around your mouth. "Use this today. The wind up there will rip your lips off."

"I'm okay," you say. You're not interested in wearing his ratty, old bandanna.

"No, really," Russ says. "It'll also help moisten the air you breathe in, which will keep you hydrated."

"*Fine*," you say, slipping on the bandanna as your team makes its way to the bottom of the Lhotse Face.

The Lhotse Face is a glittering, craggy wall of ice. There are ice cliffs and bulges every now and then. And the entire route is fixed with ropes.

Hans explains to Jake, "You must get into the rhythm of kick stepping. First, *kick* so your crampon points get stuck in the ice. Next, *step* on the foot. Then you *rest*. Kick, step, rest."

With Hans's words *Kick, step, rest* ringing in your head, you start up the first rope. You're in line between Doc and Russ. Up and up you go. It's hard work, and you pull the bandanna off your face so you can breathe more easily.

"You're doing great," Russ calls to you from below. "But keep that bandanna on your mouth! It'll protect your face and help keep you from getting dehydrated."

You slide the bandanna into place just as you arrive at—

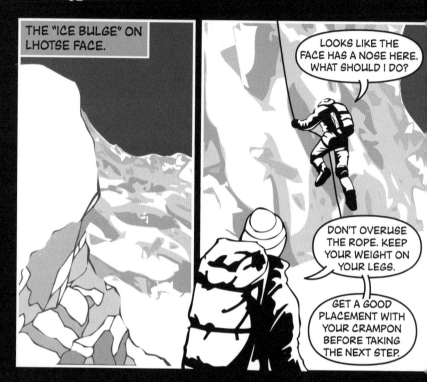

THE "ICE BULGE" ON LHOTSE FACE.

LOOKS LIKE THE FACE HAS A NOSE HERE. WHAT SHOULD I DO?

DON'T OVERUSE THE ROPE. KEEP YOUR WEIGHT ON YOUR LEGS.

GET A GOOD PLACEMENT WITH YOUR CRAMPON BEFORE TAKING THE NEXT STEP.

YOU KICK STEP AND STICK YOUR LEFT CRAMPON IN THE ICE.

UMPH!

YOU LIFT YOUR RIGHT FOOT TO DO THE SAME THING.

AND YOUR VISION BLURS.

YOU WIPE THE OUTSIDE OF THE LENS. NO GOOD. YOU CAN'T SEE!

I DON'T KNOW WHERE TO PUT MY RIGHT FOOT!

Thanks to that mouth cover Russ made you wear, the steam from your breath has totally fogged your goggles!

It's like someone has smeared thick gel on the inside of the lens. You can see light but not much else.

With one foot stuck in the ice and the other basically dangling, this is the worst time for this to happen! Your goggles are important on an icy face like this—they protect you from snow blindness. But what if you can't see anything at all—isn't that worse? What should you do?

**IF YOU TAKE OFF YOUR BLURRY GOGGLES, TURN TO PAGE 72.**

**IF YOU KEEP YOUR GOGGLES ON AND WAIT FOR THEM TO CLEAR, TURN TO PAGE 100.**

You don't have to wait long.

"Here it comes!" Russ shouts and lowers the new rope down to you. After you grab it and clip it onto your harness, Russ and Hans start pulling you up.

Soon, you're at the lip of the crevasse and Garrett is helping you out.

"So glad you could make it!" he jokes, sounding like the host of a party.

"Thanks for having me," you say, laughing as you untangle the lines and get to your feet.

After a night in Camp One, you and the team are climbing toward Camp Two.

The climb here is pretty tame, especially after the terrors of the icefall, and the team is climbing in a long line without fixed ropes.

Just as you remember that this area is sometimes called the Valley of Silence, things suddenly get really noisy.

The wind starts to howl, and . . .

SNOW IS BLOWING
EVERYWHERE.

HELLO?!
HELLO?!

WHITEOUT!

You shout some more, but it's useless. No one could ever hear you over the shrieking wind—and you can't see more than an arm's length away. Just standing still for a few minutes, the snow has already covered your feet and shins.

All signs of your tracks and those of the rest of the team? Gone, lost in the deep snow. You're alone.

*Time to make a decision. A really big one.*

You know you have all the gear that you need to wait out a whiteout like this for up to twelve hours. If it lasts longer than that, you'll be in trouble.

Or you could keep moving and find your way back to Camp One. There's no fixed line to follow, but all you'd have to do is keep walking downhill, right? How hard could that be?

Whatever you do, you better decide fast. The frozen wind is blasting into you with hurricane force!

IF YOU STAY PUT AND WAIT OUT THE WHITEOUT USING THE GEAR IN YOUR PACK, TURN TO PAGE 119.

IF YOU DECIDE TO TRY TO FIND YOUR WAY BACK TO CAMP ONE, TURN TO PAGE 116.

"*Hola*, Julia," you say, walking toward her with your plate of food. "*Bastante fria para ti*?"

You know Julia's from Argentina and might appreciate hearing some Spanish. She replies with a smile and some very fast Spanish in her Argentine accent.

"Whoa," you say. "Let me start again, in English this time: 'Hi, Julia. Cold enough for you?'"

She laughs. "Sorry! I said, 'This isn't so bad! I've been through a whole lot worse!'"

Then she tells you about when she first met Doc and Russ, climbing Aconcagua in Argentina.

"*That* was cold," she says. "But I live for snow and ice."

As you finish eating dinner, she tells you more stories about climbing through blizzard conditions, and you realize, wow, this girl is *tough*. If anyone's ready for Everest, it's Julia.

During the next week, you climb with Julia and become better friends. Eventually she lets her guard down and tells you what she finds hardest about climbing—the sleeping!

"Once I get higher up," she admits, "I have a really tough time getting any sleep."

When you reach Camp Two, you find this out firsthand. Julia can't sleep, and she keeps you awake, talking. You don't get to bed until 2:00 a.m.

→

"Wake up," Russ calls, tapping on your tent. "You overslept. We're climbing the Lhotse Face this morning."

Blearily, you open your eyes. Your head is pounding.

"Okay, Russ, I'm awake," you say. Once he leaves, though, you fall right back to sleep.

→

Russ wakes you up—again—twenty minutes later, and he's not happy. When you stumble out of your tent, you still don't feel right. Your head and stomach ache. You see Julia standing with the rest of the team, also rubbing her eyes.

"You and Julia have kept the team waiting," Russ says. "Now we're running an hour behind schedule. If we're going to leave, we have to go now."

Julia says she's tired but ready. What about you?

You're not used to seeing Russ upset. You'd like to make him happy and prove that you're a good mountaineer. But are you feeling up to the climb?

**IF YOU STAY AT CAMP TWO UNTIL THE NEXT DAY, TURN TO PAGE 130.**

**IF YOU START THE DAY'S CLIMB LATE, TURN TO PAGE 141.**

"I can't see!" you shout.

This is terrifying. Like a nightmare. You're hanging by one foot from the Lhotse Face—and nearly blind.

"Don't move!" Doc shouts from above.

"I can't hang on!" you yell. "My—"

*Crink!* The small sound cuts through the wind and grabs your attention. The point of your one stable crampon is now slipping out of the ice.

You're clipped to the rope, but falling now would mean smashing onto the face and possibly breaking a couple bones.

A blurry figure appears in front of you. "Put a hand on my shoulder," a voice says. It's Doc. "I'm right here."

You try, and your crampon breaks free. Suddenly, you're sliding back. Then a strong arm presses up against your back, holding you in place. That's Russ.

"Right behind you," he says. "Just move your feet when and where I tell you."

For the next five minutes, Russ supports your back and gives you step-by-step instructions—literally. Together the three of you move as one, and suddenly, you're off the bulge and on level ground. You slump in relief.

"We're not out of the woods yet," Doc says. "We still have a short hike to Camp Three. Breathe really hard through the bandanna, and your goggles should defog."

You're gasping for air after that climb, but you give it a shot. Soon you can see again, and the world has never looked better. You're even happy to see Hans's face.

Ten minutes later, the team finally reaches Camp Three. Lhakpa has been there for a day with the Sherpas setting up camp. He greets you warmly and then chuckles at your huffing and puffing. "It's okay, my friend. You can stop breathing so hard into your mask. You've arrived safely and all is well."

→

Lhakpa is right. All *is* well. After a night at Camp Three, the team returns to Base Camp to rest.

A week later, you're approaching Camp Three again. The plan is to head to Camp Four the next night and then summit the day after. Your utlimate goal is just days away!

Just then, though, things start to go wrong.

Worn out from the climb, the rest of the team ducks into their tents except for you and Julia. Outside her tent, she's coughing. Her whole body jerks with the force of it.

"Are you okay?" you ask. "You could crack a rib with that coughing, or it could be something worse. We better tell Doc."

Julia holds up a hand. "I'm okay. This just happens sometimes, even back home. You know Doc. If you tell her, she'll get all worried and send me down to Base Camp. Then I'll miss out on the summit window—for nothing!"

She'll be fine. Probably just needs some rest. And Doc *is* pretty cautious. Even if it's minor, she might send Julia down the mountain just to be safe. Or—is Julia really sick?

**IF YOU TELL DOC ABOUT JULIA, TURN TO PAGE 111.**

**IF YOU DON'T TELL DOC, TURN TO PAGE 109.**

You make your way over to Hans and stand next to him as he wolfs down huge spoonfuls of *dal bhat*. Soon he sets down his plate, pulls out a slim device, and starts skimming through some kind of eBook. Before he can walk away, you ask:

"What are you reading?"

With a sigh, he holds the screen toward you. The page from the book has a photograph of a man who looks familiar. But the text is in German. "I can't read that."

Hans gives you a cold look with his blue eyes, as if the fact you can't read German is just one more reason why you shouldn't be climbing Everest.

Then you know why the man in the photo looks familiar. "That's Sir Edmund Hillary," you say. Hillary and the Sherpa Tenzing Norgay were the first people to successfully summit and descend from Mount Everest in 1953.

Hans shrugs. "Most people know about Hillary," he says.

"And that book is *High Adventure*, the story of his Everest climb," you say. "I've read it. Well, the English version anyway."

"Really," Hans replies quietly.

Have you finally managed to impress him?

Hans finishes eating and says, "My grandfather climbed with Hillary once."

"That's amazing," you say. "Your dad is a mountain climber, too, right?"

Hans nods. "One of the world's greatest."

"Must be tough to feel like you're living in the shadow of your dad and grandfather," you say. "Is that why you're climbing without supplemental oxygen?"

Hans looks at you with squinty eyes. "I'm doing it because I like challenges," he says.

"Has your dad or your grandfather summited Everest without oxygen?" you ask.

"No," he says. "I will be the first."

You have a feeling Hans *is* trying to prove something— but he's never going to admit it to *you.*

Changing the subject, Hans says, "Have a look at this."

He clicks to a photo app on his device. He taps a slide-show button, and incredible photos start popping up on the screen. There's Hans at the summit of K2. There he is at the top of Denali. Then at the peak of Makalu.

"These pictures are amazing," you tell him.

"Whenever I climb, I take many photos," Hans says. "My friends and family love my slideshows."

You think of your camera, which has been buried in your pack, and you make a plan to use it a lot more.

→

A week after your meal with Hans, you and the team are on your way to Camp Two. The climb isn't steep, but you're using fixed ropes to be safe, in case there are hidden crevasses.

You've had a few more talks with Hans and feel like you're getting to know him better. In fact, Hans is climbing right behind you, giving you little pointers here and there.

On a break, he asks, "Do you know why this is called the Western Cwm?"

You laugh. "I don't even know what a *cwm* is."

"It's pronounced *coom*, and it's a Welsh word for valley," Hans says with the hint of a smile. "This is also sometimes called the Valley of Silence. It has great views! And there's a great place for a picture just off the route."

The next thing you know, Hans is unclipping from the fixed rope.

"You can come if you want," he says, "and we'll take a photo for *your* slideshow."

**IF YOU UNCLIP TO GO WITH HANS, TURN TO PAGE 59.**

**IF YOU STAY ON THE FIXED ROPE AND SKIP THE PIC, TURN TO PAGE 137.**

"Wait!" Julia says. "What are you doing?"

"Stop!" Doc shouts, when she sees you unclipped from the fixed rope.

But you can't stop now. You've got to pee, and you can't wait. You rush off the route, down a slightly icy slope, looking for some privacy.

Just one more step ought to put you out of everyone's view. Your foot comes down. It keeps going . . . and going . . . as you break through a paper-thin layer of snow and drop into a two-story crevasse below.

Screaming, you fall through space. Your outstretched leg hits the bottom first with a snap that says it all: You've broken your leg.

"Hold on!" Russ calls from above. "I'm coming for you."

Hans and Doc lower Russ down. He creates a harness out of rope, and the others pull you up. They're careful, but you spin, and your broken leg hits the wall of the crevasse.

The pain shoots through your body, but this lift is smooth sailing compared to your next mode of transportation. A yak will be your ride back to Lukla from Base Camp. You're going home—and all because you couldn't wait to *go*.

**THE END**

"What's up, Garrett?" you ask as you stroll toward him with your plate of food.

Before answering, the Australian spears a piece of grilled meat with his fork and looks at it carefully. "Now, what do you figure this used to be?"

"As long as it wasn't yak," you say, "I'm fine with it."

"Back in Sydney, my family and I grill all the time. As long as you slather enough sauce on something, it's good. But I don't think all the sauce in the world could save this piece of shoe leather." Garrett shrugs and puts the meat in his mouth and chews for a second. "*Hmm.* You know, it's pretty good, actually." He gives the Sherpa in charge of cooking the meal a wave. "Compliments to the chef!"

You wave, too, as the Sherpa plays along and takes a little bow. Then you ask Garrett: "How'd a city kid like you get into mountain climbing?"

"I was always a bit of a practical jokester," he says. "You know, the usual stuff. Toads under Dad's pillow or fake vomit on my teacher's chair." Garrett chuckles. "My folks thought I had a little too much energy. What better way to burn it off than by climbing a mountain or two? They sent me for my first climb with Russ and Doc when I was ten. We went up Mount Aspiring in New Zealand, and I was instantly hooked on climbing. Now my parents are happy. I'm happy. Worked out great."

"So, you're done with the kidding around?" you ask.

"I'm always ready for a good joke, you know that," he says. "But when it comes to reaching the summit of Everest, I'm all business. It's the most important thing I've ever done." And, from the look in his eyes, he's definitely not kidding. After a second, Garrett's face breaks into a grin. "Well, that was a heavy moment, wasn't it? Let's eat up—don't want to talk ourselves out. Especially because it looks like we'll be sharing a tent tonight."

After dinner, the two of you are getting ready for bed in your tent. Facing away from you, Garrett is taking off his boots, and you're making a little pillow out of your jacket. "Lucky for me there aren't any toads this high," you say to Garrett. "Otherwise, who knows what you'd put under my—"

"Ouch," Garrett says and the sound of pain in his voice makes you stop.

"Something wrong?" you ask, glancing over his shoulder at his now bare feet.

What you see makes you gasp in shock.

**TURN TO PAGE 140.**

The next morning, the whole team has on their gear, ready to leave Camp Three. You're just waiting for Russ to get the final weather report. When he comes out of his tent, he says that the wind will be picking up during the day.

"If we weren't all healthy," he continues, "I'd say let's wait a day. But the team is strong, so I say we make the climb to Camp Four today and prepare to summit."

You glance at Julia, wondering if she'll speak up. She doesn't. Later, as you're climbing, she starts coughing a lot. No one can hear her over the sound of the wind except you.

Then, just as you're approaching Camp Four, Julia stumbles and falls. You and Doc rush to her, and when you find she can't walk on her own, you both help her to her tent.

After examining Julia, Doc whispers to you, "She has HAPE—high-altitude pulmonary edema. Her lungs are filling with water, and she's not getting enough oxygen. I need to get her down the mountain. We'll start out before dawn."

That night, you're too worried about Julia to sleep—and then you hear her voice outside your tent!

You rush outside and, in the moonlight, you see Julia hobbling away from camp, wheezing. You run to her just as she says, "I need fresh air! I can't breathe!"

"Doc!" you shout. "Russ! Help!"

Julia is stumbling as she walks, and there's a six-story drop only steps away. You reach for Julia and catch her just in time. Whew, that was a close one.

*Crack!*

The sheet of ice under you breaks and slants down. You and Julia are now slipping straight for the drop. Julia starts screaming in Spanish. As you fall through the air, you realize what she's saying—*Ayúdanos!*

And you realize that no amount of *ayuda* will get you out of this one.

**THE END**

After you tell Doc, she is by Julia's side in a flash.

"That sounds like it could be a chest infection," Doc announces after a quick examination. "We need to get this under control. I have to get Julia back down to Base Camp right away."

Between coughs, Julia gives you an angry look. "See what you've done? I thought you were my friend!"

"I'm sorry," you say, but Julia won't even speak to you.

It's hard to blame her. Because of your decision to tell Doc, Julia probably won't be able to summit with you and the rest of the team.

The next morning, as Doc prepares to take Julia down the mountain, you overhear Russ and Doc talking.

"The rest of us are heading back down to Camp Two," Russ says. "The weather up above is just too lousy, and it's not supposed to clear for two days. That's when we'll make the decision about heading to Camp Four and summiting—with or without you two. Radio me with updates. And please be careful!"

"I will," Doc says and gives him a kiss good-bye.

After Julia and Doc have left, you and the rest of the team make your way down to Camp Two. There, you pass the time by reading, listening to music, and playing checkers with Garrett. But the thin air leaves you tired and out of sorts. It's hard to do anything but worry about Julia. You really hope she'll be okay.

By the time evening rolls around, you're really starting to go stir-crazy just as Russ sticks his head inside your tent.

"Good news," he says. "Doc just radioed. They've reached Base Camp."

"How's Julia?" you ask.

"They had to stop a lot because of her coughing fits. But now she's safe in a warm bed," Russ assures you. "Compared to the high camps, Base Camp is like a fancy hotel."

You're glad Julia's safe. But will she get better in time to summit with you? *Come on, Julia. Get back up here.*

$$\longrightarrow$$

You're still at Camp Two two days later. The weather has kept you from climbing, but you can't stay this high much longer. If the weather improves, the plan is to leave for Camp Three tomorrow. Then you'll head to Camp Four the next day, and finally, reach the summit the day after that—*without* Julia and Doc.

You're in Russ's tent waiting for a weather report when Doc's voice comes crackling over the radio. She announces that Julia's chest is clear!

RUSS?
IT'S DOC...

"If she stays healthy," Doc says, "we'll head back up tomorrow and join you. She seems strong, so I'm optimistic."

"We'll wait for you," Russ says. He signs off and turns to you with a grin. "You did good," he says. "I'm proud of you for watching out for your teammate." Then, of course, he puts you in a headlock.

Two days later, Julia, Doc, and the two Sherpas arrive back in Camp Two. Julia looks tired from the climb. But her color is back. And the cough is gone.

"Ah! It lives!" Garrett shouts when he spots Julia. Julia gives him a playful swat, and then Garrett drags you both into a big bear hug as if you're all best buddies.

But are you?

As if to answer that question, Julia takes you aside. She gives you a bright smile. "Thanks for telling Doc about my cough. Turns out you really are my friend."

Together again, you and the team spend the next night in Camp Three and head out for Camp Four in the morning. From now on, everyone—except Hans—will wear an oxygen mask. Your mask is uncomfortable at first, and it makes it tough to talk to others, but you're *very* glad you have it.

Six hours after leaving Camp Three, Russ shouts to you over the whipping wind, "Welcome to Camp Four!"

At Camp Four, conditions are beyond miserable. The biting wind has really picked up and cuts into any bare patch of skin like a knife.

This is the Death Zone—where oxygen is extremely thin and bodies literally start dying. Russ calls for a team meeting to decide whether you'll head for the summit that night.

"Can we get this thing done already?" Jake asks before Russ can even speak. "I'm sitting on a frozen butt here!"

Russ looks at the sky. With the wind gusts spitting up snow, it's hard to see the top of Everest. "It's not perfect, that's for sure," he says. "But the climb is doable, and it might not get any better this season. In fact, it might get worse."

"So could our health if we stay here too long," Hans adds. He's the only one not wearing an oxygen mask, so his voice is the clearest. "Sometimes you only get one shot."

Russ thinks it over and finally says, "Okay, we go tonight."

"Yes!" Julia shouts.

"Youngest team to summit!" Garrett says. "This is it!"

But you're not celebrating. You've got this sickening feeling in your gut and a pounding headache. Both started yesterday when you arrived and only got worse overnight.

"I'm not sure about climbing tonight," you say and wince. Even talking makes your head pound more.

Hans rolls his eyes. "You're probably just scared—"

"Sure, I'm scared," you interrupt. "We all are. But that's not it. I have a splitting headache and I feel really nauseous. I think my body is telling me it just isn't the day."

After a second, you look at Doc and add, "Maybe I need to wait for the right wave."

Hans steps closer to you. "We *all* feel nauseous and we *all* have headaches. That's what happens when you're up this high. It *hurts*."

Doc holds up a hand to quiet Hans, then asks you, "Have you been eating?"

"Not really," you say. "A few spoonfuls of oatmeal. I couldn't get much more down without gagging."

Hans rolls his eyes again. "Ask yourself if it's really your *body* that's having trouble, or if it's your *mind*."

Fair question. Maybe today *is* your one shot at making the summit. Tomorrow the weather could be much worse.

**IF YOU DECIDE TO ATTEMPT TO SUMMIT WITH THE GROUP, TURN TO PAGE 148.**

**IF YOU GIVE UP THIS CHANCE TO CLIMB WITH THE YOUNGEST TEAM TO EVER SUMMIT EVEREST, TURN TO PAGE 123.**

*Okay. Camp One, here I come.*

You start walking in the direction you think is downhill. It's actually trickier than you'd think to figure out which way is down. The heaps of blowing, drifting snow make it hard to determine the sloping ground, and you still can't see a thing. All you see is bright, glowing white, all around you.

Still, on and on you plod through deep snow. Each step, you have to lift your leg as high as you can.

"Help!" you yell. "Help!"

*Get a grip.* You tell yourself, forcing your mouth shut. *You're freaking out. This is how people start making bad decisions, and this is how they . . .*

You can't finish the thought. You're not going to think negative stuff like that. You made a decision to find Camp One, and you're going to stick to the plan.

Hours later, you're beyond exhausted, cold to your bones, and

moving very slowly. For a brief second, the clouds partially clear, and the sun pops out above you.

Then it's gone. And the whiteout is back in full force.

Wait, you think. Was that really just the sun in the sky? Or was it light reflecting off something at Camp One? Could safety be that close?

You start running—well, you can't run in the snow, so it's more like shuffling—toward where you saw the light. You're huffing and wheezing, but you're going to make it. You can picture your warm sleeping bag and a hot bowl of soup.

"Here I come!" you shout.

Then there's the strangest sensation. Your feet are no longer on the ground. And it's easier to move.

In a split second, you know why. You're falling. You must have stumbled into a crevasse, and now you're rocketing down into the hole. And judging from the time it's taking to fall, you know you're not going to survive the landing.

*Oomph!*

Just as you hit the bottom, you see another light. Only this one appears to be a very different kind of light, and it's at the end of a very long tunnel . . . .

**THE END**

When you come back to your tent with Doc, Garrett is still kicking his feet against the ice. He stops when he sees Doc and snaps at you, "I asked you not to tell her!"

Doc calms him down and looks at his feet. "This is serious frostbite," she says. "If we're going to save your toes, we need to get you to a hospital. I'll take you down to Base Camp tomorrow and then have a helicopter evacuate you."

"I'm sorry," you say to Garrett when Doc leaves.

Garrett's had time to cool down. "I know that, mate. I just can't believe I won't be at the summit with you and Julia."

You're sure you made the right decision. Doc and Russ keep telling you that. It doesn't make it any easier, though, when you have to wave good-bye to Garrett when he leaves with Doc in the morning. You're going to miss him.

Four days later, Doc rejoins the expedition after seeing Garrett safely to the hospital, where his parents met them.

Then, for the next few weeks, it's countless grueling climbs in blistering cold—and then you reach Camp Four.

**TURN TO PAGE 144.**

*All right, if I'm going to stay put, I might as well get a little more comfortable.*

Comfortable in a whiteout on Mount Everest? Yeah, right. But you do need to get out of the wind if you can.

You grab your ice axe and begin digging a trench in the snow. It's hard work, and after a half hour of digging, you're exhausted. But you've made progress.

You put your pack in the bottom of the trench and lay on it to prevent the snow from absorbing too much of your body heat. And then you hunker down, taking bites of a protein bar to keep up your energy. This is the crudest kind of shelter. Basically a long, shallow hole.

But it might just save your life.

$\longrightarrow$

You survived! Six hours after it came crashing into your team, the whiteout finally lifts. Now the sun is setting. Soon, darkness will fall—and so will temperatures. You need to find your way back to Camp One.

Just as you start out around an outcropping of rock and ice, you hear something and freeze. *What was that?*

Then you hear it again. It's Russ calling your name!

"Russ!" you shout. "I'm over here!"

Russ and Hans come around the outcropping. Rushing over to you, Russ throws his arms around you. "We've been looking for you!"

After making sure you're okay, Russ explains, "The rest of us rode out the storm in the valley, too. I was with Hans and Jake. And Doc was with Garrett and Julia. You were the only one alone. And you made it. I'm really proud of you!"

You're not sorry Russ's praise makes you blush—the heat rushing to your frozen cheeks feels great.

You can't sleep. Could be the altitude. Could be nerves.

Four weeks after you survived the whiteout—and several trips back to Base Camp—it's midnight, and you're in your tent perched on the side of Everest at Camp Three. Tomorrow you will head to Camp Four and then the summit!

No wonder you can't sleep.

Outside it's quiet, for once. After the constant wind and blowing snow of the past few weeks, the silence seems so strange. You go out to take a look.

Sure, you knew a trip to Everest would be full of heart-pounding action. But you never thought it'd also be so insanely beautiful.

After a few minutes of staring at the stars sparkling in the clear sky, you head back to your tent.

You slip off your boots, keeping the inner lining on for warmth. Just as you're climbing into your sleeping bag, there's a rumbling outside. This can mean only one thing—

Avalanche!

And it sounds like it's heading straight for your camp. Your brain kicks into high gear. You have seconds—if that long—to come up with a plan.

**IF YOU STAY IN YOUR TENT AND HOPE THE AVALANCHE MISSES YOU, TURN TO PAGE 127.**

**IF YOU RUN OUT OF YOUR TENT, TURN TO PAGE 129.**

"I'm waiting here," you say. "I'm not going to summit today."

There's a pause.

"Very funny." Garrett chuckles, adjusting his goggles. "Now let's go get ready to climb."

But you don't give in. "I'm serious. I'm not feeling well, and I'm staying here."

This stops Russ in his tracks. He turns to look at you and then announces, "Everyone in my tent. Dorjee, can you join us, please?"

It's crowded in Russ's tent with eight people in there.

Jake glares at you. "We've been stuck up on this mountain waiting for weeks for this, and now you want us to wait some more? It's time to win this game!"

"I'm sorry," you reply. "But this isn't a game. This is real."

"I'll tell you what's real," Jake points an angry finger at you. "The risk of death up here is real. We're getting weaker by the second!"

"We'll be okay for one more night, right, Russ?" you ask.

Russ nods. "Yes, we have enough oxygen to stay another night."

Jake isn't having any of this. He snaps. "We can't spend another night here. No way. We have to go now!"

His words hang in the air for a minute. Finally, Julia looks at you and says, "I'm not going without you."

Then Garrett says, "I'll wait for you, too."

Russ leans closer to Dorjee Sherpa. Doc joins them. After a moment, Russ turns back to the rest of the team. "All right, it's settled. We'll wait until tomorrow."

Dorjee gives you a nod as he leaves the tent. Is he telling you he respects your decision? You can't be sure.

"Youngest team?" Jake throws his hands in the air. "Why didn't I sponsor the *oldest* team to ever summit Everest?"

You can tell Jake's angry. But at least his joke shows he's still part of the team.

The rest of that day and the start of the next day are beyond miserable. You hang out in your tent with Julia and Garrett. You're all wearing oxygen masks, lying down to conserve energy, and trying to stay warm. Every once in a while you eat some oatmeal and drink a little water, but it all tastes terrible at this high altitude.

$\rightarrow$

That afternoon, you go to bed at 4:00 p.m.—Russ's orders— but the screaming wind keeps you awake. It's almost like it's yelling at you for missing your appointment at the summit that day.

You unzip the tent at 8:00 p.m. and push the snow aside to get out. Russ is up, and he gives you the night's forecast.

"The winds have died down and visibility is good," he says. "How about you? How're you feeling?"

"Headache's still there but not as bad at all," you say. "Stomach's a little upset but nothing I can't deal with."

Russ nods. "Excellent."

With brains and bodies that have slowed down thanks to lack of oxygen, it takes more than two hours for everyone to eat breakfast and get their gear on. But finally, at 10:30 p.m., you're all set!

Just then Doc steps in front of you. "Have you been hydrating?" she demands. "You need to drink at least two liters of water before the climb."

*Annoying!* You spent the afternoon forcing down a liter of water. You're not thirsty at all and just want to get going! Plus, you've already experienced what it was like to have a full bladder while climbing in the icefall. Not good. There will be no safe time or place for a pee break tonight.

**IF YOU DRINK EVEN MORE WATER, TURN TO PAGE 164.**

**IF YOU DECIDE YOU'VE HAD ENOUGH WATER, TURN TO PAGE 159.**

As you sit alone in your tent, terrified, the rumble of the approaching avalanche gets louder. And louder. Until it seems like a line of locomotives must be barreling down the mountain—straight at you. You've never been so scared or felt so helpless in your life.

The ice hits first. And then chunks of snow. The wind created by all that rushing snow and ice reminds you of the air shooting out the back of a jet engine. You don't think your tent's anchors can hold against this onlaught. The sides are flapping violently, and you feel the bottom lifting, like the tent might take off with you still inside.

"Ahhhhh!" someone screams.

And you realize it's you! You close your mouth as the ice under you continues to shake and move. You're gripping your sleeping bag hard.

Then . . .

It's quiet.

The avalanche just nicked your camp. It's over.

"Everyone all right?" It's Russ, and he's out of his tent. You unzip yours and join him outside.

Blocks of ice and piles of snow are scattered here and there—a reminder of how close your camp came to being dinner for a hungry avalanche. Jake's tent took the worst hit—one side has been ripped open by a huge block of ice. But he's okay. He gives Hans a high five, happy to be alive.

Garrett and Julia are out there grinning like crazy, too, and you all share a group hug.

"Did anyone get the license plate of that truck that came barreling through here?" Doc says, making a joke. And even though it's not a very good one, you all laugh. You're a little hysterical after that brush with disaster.

After you've helped Jake get his tent set back up, Russ says, "Okay, let's try to get a couple more hours of sleep. Tomorrow we leave for Camp Four."

**TURN TO PAGE 144.**

No time to grab your jacket or your boots. You burst out into the frozen night air. The rumbling sound grows louder. You have to warn the others! You start shouting, "Avalanche! Avalanche! Aval—ahh!"

You've stepped onto an icy slope at the edge of camp, and suddenly you're sliding. The boot liners have no traction on the ice—you might as well be wearing greased skis.

*This isn't good,* you think as you fall on your butt and start sliding down the dark Lhotse Face. Soon you're racing so fast over a steep ice cliff, you doubt that even the avalanche could catch you.

**THE END**

"Sorry, Russ," you say. "I need to stick around here today. I'm just not feeling up for the climb."

After a quick discussion with Doc, Russ tells you, "All right, Doc will wait here with you. You can catch up with us tomorrow."

Just like that, no guilt, no criticism. You know you made the right choice!

Each day over the next two weeks, as you and the team ascend a little higher and then return to Base Camp to rest, your body is getting more and more used to the altitude.

But it's strange—while your blood cells might be better equipped to deal with the thin air now, the altitude is taking its toll on you and the rest of the team in other ways.

For one thing, food doesn't taste that good anymore, and people are losing weight. Your faces are red and puffy from exposure to the cold and sun.

And no one sleeps well anymore, especially Julia. You find out she's always struggled with sleep at high altitudes. Fortunately, Doc has been giving her some herbal tea each night. That's helped her drop off for a few hours.

Then, finally! After all the weeks of climbing and struggle, it looks like the brutal ascent might almost be over: You've reached Camp Four.

The whining sound of the wind outside your flapping tent is nonstop here at Camp Four. That noise—and the waiting—is enough to make you half crazy. You were hoping to climb to the summit last night, but the weather was just too nasty.

*I can't take it anymore.*

And you're not alone. It's the afternoon after your arrival at Camp Four, and the team has about reached its limits. Something's got to give. Either the weather has to improve so you can summit tonight, or you'll have to head back down.

One day—two at most—is pretty much as long as you want to hang out up here. There's a reason that they call this part of Everest the Death Zone. You're wearing an oxygen mask, but it's still not enough to fight the thin air—and your body is literally dying, little by little. Your brain's slowing down.

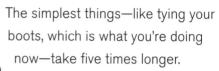

The simplest things—like tying your boots, which is what you're doing now—take five times longer.

You stop and look at your fingertips. Seven out of ten are super white, like the color of milk. And the others are red and looked burned. It's pretty obvious what it is: *Frostbite.*

An hour later, you've all jammed into Russ and Doc's tent to listen to the weather report. It's clearing on the summit—but only a little.

"Okay," Russ says. "It's not perfect, but it's the best we can hope for. We'll climb to the summit tonight."

The others smile and Jake even lets out a Texas whoop. Your brain, though, is a little too fuzzy to celebrate and you think it'd probably hurt the frostbite on your fingers to give anyone a high five.

"What's wrong?" Russ asks you. "Aren't you ready to climb tonight?"

**IF YOU DECIDE IT'S TIME TO SUMMIT, TURN TO PAGE 70.**

**IF YOU THINK YOU BETTER GIVE UP ON THE CLIMB BECAUSE OF YOUR FROSTBITE, TURN TO PAGE 146.**

When you wake up from your nap, you feel don't feel any better. In fact, you actually feel *more* tired than you did before. As the sun sets, your head starts pounding, and it's really hard to get to sleep that night.

The next day is supposed to be a "rest day" at Camp Two, so you spend a lot of time lying in your tent, trying to sleep. But it's not easy to nap when your head is still pounding, despite all the headache medicine Doc gives you.

By the time your third day at Camp Two rolls around, you know something's *really* wrong when you step out of your tent and find it hard to walk toward the dining tent.

Doc reaches for you. "Can you walk a straight line?"

"Um, I don't know," you slur and fall over.

After examining you, Doc explains you have the early signs of HACE—high-altitude cerebral edema. Simply put, your brain is swelling. Doc gives you medicine to help, but they need to get you down the mountain and to a hospital as soon as possible.

Your climb is over.

And your only souvenir? A really bad headache that will last for weeks.

**THE END**

THE NEXT MORNING YOU'RE CLIMBING TOWARD CAMP TWO.

GARRETT SEEMS FINE.

THEN YOU NOTICE HIM KICKING THE SNOW.

I CAN'T FEEL MY TOES!

YOU APPROACH HIM.

LET'S TELL DOC.

Trying to help Garrett, you land on the front spike of his crampon. It digs into your knee. You fall to the ice, moaning, lying next to Garrett.

"Are you two okay?" Doc calls down to you as the rest of the team gathers at the rim of the shallow crevasse.

Garrett shouts, "I think I broke my ankle!"

You can't really talk right now—the pain in your knee is that bad. You think you might even pass out, watching your blood gush onto the snow.

Doc and Russ lower themselves down to you. A quick examination, and it's clear that you and Garrett are headed back to Base Camp and that your trip to the summit is over. By the time you heal, the climbing season will have ended.

It's enough to make you want to pass out, just so you don't have to think about it.

And sure enough, when you catch sight of the deep gash in your knee, you get your wish.

**THE END**

Unclipping from the fixed rope just to take a picture for a slideshow? *Hmm*, that doesn't sound like the best plan—and you're sure Doc and Russ would have something to say about that.

"Thanks, Hans," you tell him. "A picture might be worth a thousand words—but not my life."

"Suit yourself!" he calls back, shaking his head, disappointed in you. "It'll be hard to have a slideshow with no pictures!"

It's clear the bond you've been forming with Hans takes a hit. But at least by staying clipped onto the fixed rope, you'll be around to enjoy the summit.

You catch up with Garrett and Julia, who are climbing just behind Russ.

"It's the third brave young passenger!" Julia says with a smile when she sees you.

Garrett gives you a friendly salute, and then says, "Russ was just telling us to stay on the route and on the ropes. The sun is making the icy surface feel like a greased pan."

You glance back down the long, sloping valley. Hans is heading back to the rope after taking his picture. He almost slips, recovers, and then clips back into the rope. You wonder, though, if you would've been able to keep your balance.

It's the team's first night in Camp Two. You're sharing a tent with Jake, who is snoring loudly in his sleeping bag. Lucky guy.

The high altitude and the whining wind make it tricky for you to fall asleep—so you're writing in your journal:

*The Sherpas were here before us and set up our camp. Had a good meal. Really happy I'm here, but we've been in Nepal for about a month now, and I miss home a little, especially at night. And nights seem longer as we get closer to the top. I'm just anxious about the climb, and—*

"What's up?" Jake asks you, breaking into your thoughts and rubbing his eyes. He's suddenly awake. "Can't sleep?"

"Not really," you say.

Jake seems pretty sleepy, but he pulls out a deck of cards. "Let's play a hand or two and chew the fat. Always helps me catch some Zs. Besides, what kind of expedition sponsor would I be if I didn't make sure our climbers are at their best?"

You play cards for about five minutes—and that's all it takes. You're exhausted. As you put your head down and start to drift off, you mumble sleepily, "Thanks, Jake."

"This trip really has its ups and downs, doesn't it?" Julia says to you two weeks later.

You've got to agree— that's a great way to describe your ascent.

After each climb toward the top of Everest, you have to return to Base Camp to rest. Then you go back up the mountain again—always a little higher. It's a slow process, but you can feel yourself getting stronger in the thin air. By the time you reach Camp Three, you know your body is churning out all the extra red blood cells you'll need to make the summit.

And you're going to need all the strength you can get. Why? The next day you're heading to Camp Four. This will be your second trip there. The first time, bad weather kept you from reaching the summit, and you had to come back down.

Tomorrow you'll try again. So brace yourself— You're about to head into the Death Zone.

**TURN TO PAGE 157.**

*That looks like frostbite.*

The last three toes on one of Garrett's feet are scary. They're grayish, and they have blisters popping up here and there. *How has he even been able to walk?*

Garrett sees you looking at his feet and covers them up.

"That could be frostbite," you say.

Garrett shakes his head. "Really bad frostbite is black, my feet are just kind of pale. I'm fine. I just have to wear an extra pair of socks to keep my feet warmer."

"You were already wearing two pairs," you say. "This could be serious. Let's tell Doc."

"No, she might send me back to Base Camp!" he shouts. Then he says more quietly, "Like I said, nothing is more important to me than reaching the summit of Mount Everest. For once, I want to be taken seriously."

As you think about what to do, Garrett starts kicking his feet against the floor of the tent. "This should get the blood flowing again! And all will be right as rain, you'll see!"

**IF YOU TELL DOC ABOUT GARRETT'S FEET, TURN TO PAGE 118.**

**IF YOU AGREE WITH GARRETT THAT HE'S FINE, TURN TO PAGE 134.**

"Hope you're really ready for this," Doc warns you and Julia when your team reaches the bottom of the Lhotse Face.

"Holy cow," you say, looking up. The face is like a skyscraper made of hard blue ice. A fixed rope has been installed on the face, running along a path that's pretty easy to spot, thanks to the other teams who've climbed before you.

Russ points out that you'll really make use of your carabiners today.

"When you get to an anchor," Russ says, referring to a spot where the fixed rope is anchored to the face, "you'll need to clip a carabiner above the anchor before unclipping the second carabiner. That way, you'll always be on a fixed rope and won't risk falling down the face."

As you climb behind Russ, each inch up the mountain is a challenge. You have to kick the point of one crampon into the ice. Then step up and kick into the ice with

your other foot. And repeat over and over and over. It takes a ton of strength.

An hour later, Russ calls out, "Traffic jam!"

You have your head down, concentrating on your kick stepping, so you think you must have misheard him. A traffic jam on Mount Everest?

You look up.

A long line of French climbers you recognize from Base Camp is coming down the face. They're clipped onto the same rope you are. You're going up and they're coming down.

Russ is right. It *is* a traffic jam. And it's going to add time to your climb. You're feeling tired and hot—and you just want to get this day over with already!

Russ meets up with the first descending climber and says hello in French.

Then, as he moves around the Frenchman, he calls instructions back to you: "When you get close to the climber coming down, move to your right. Make sure your feet are secure. Unclip your carabiner. Reach around the climber and reclip to the line."

*Okay*, you think to yourself. *Got it.*

When you come face-to-face with the first French climber, you give him a nod.

*Here we go*, you say to yourself.

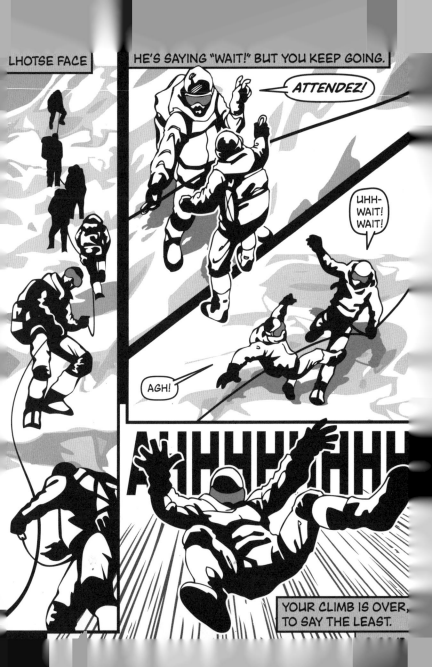

*Wow, that's a lot of people.*

You and Julia are standing outside your tent at Camp Four, amazed by the mass of other tents that clings to the side of the mountain.

Your team arrived up here this afternoon, hoping for the weather to clear so you can start your climb to the top of Everest tonight. And while you've been waiting, more and more climbers have been showing up. Now it's a regular climber convention!

There are close to a hundred climbers from teams from around the world—all with different customs and different languages.

But you share one thing in common: You're desperately hoping for the weather to get better so you can summit.

"How are we all going to fit along the narrow route to

the summit at the same time?" Julia asks, her words muffled through her oxygen mask. Up here in the dangerously thin air of Camp Four, the whole team is wearing masks—except for Hans, of course, who still wants to prove he can summit without supplemental oxygen.

And tonight might be his chance. The clouds have just rolled away and the sun is blazing in the sky—at least for now.

You can see all the other climbers gathering their things, preparing for the climb at the same time. No one wants to spend a night in the miserable—possibly deadly—cold of Camp Four if they don't have to. For some reason, all the movement makes you think of a bottle filled with ice cubes—and how all those cubes can clog up the neck and stop the liquid from flowing through.

"Good news," Jake says, joining you and Julia. "Russ thinks the weather will hold and we can climb tonight. We'll be at the summit soon!"

You point out all the people who have the same plan.

"The more the merrier!" Jake says. "I'm not waiting for the crowds to thin out. Let's go get our gear together!"

**IF YOU WAIT TO TRY FOR THE SUMMIT TOMORROW, WHEN THERE MIGHT BE FEWER PEOPLE, TURN TO PAGE 170.**

**IF YOU DECIDE TODAY IS THE DAY TO SUMMIT, TURN TO PAGE 182.**

No question about it, this is the toughest decision you've ever made.

"I'm not going to summit," you tell the others, having a hard time at first even saying the words. Then with more determination, you say, "I'm going down."

You look each team member in the eye. You want them to know you mean what you say. Russ and Doc both nod.

"Come on," Jake says. "You can beat this mountain!"

"This trip shouldn't be about conquering Everest," you tell him. "It's about respecting its power."

Jake opens his mouth to argue, but then closes it, like he's thinking about what you just said.

Of course, you let Lhakpa know that he definitely should go ahead and summit if he wants. But he shakes his head. "I believe you are right about this. I'll go down with you."

And, one by one, the others come around to your way of thinking. The last holdout is Hans. He checks out the darkening sky and finally shrugs. "This just isn't meant to be right now."

The next morning, after listening to the radio, Russ tells you that the blizzard conditions at the top of Everest reached record-breaking wind speeds and low visibility yesterday—exactly when you would have reached the summit.

You and the team feel like you've dodged a bullet. The others give you high fives and hug you, calling you a hero for having the wisdom not to summit.

Unfortunately, the weather pattern is predicted to hold for the next ten days, so it looks like there will be no more good climbing days this season.

"We may have missed our chance this time," Julia says. "But at least we still have the chance to come back again next year!"

Russ shushes all of you as more reports come over the radio. Other expeditions on the mountain weren't as lucky as yours. A few teams stubbornly pushed ahead through the bad weather, and a team from Belgium lost three climbers, and a team from Japan lost two.

"Let's take some time to think about those climbers," Russ says, "and honor their memory."

You are all quiet for a moment.

Later, you go outside to gaze at Mount Everest. The distant summit is hidden in swirling gray clouds. But you know you'll see it again, don't you?

Because you'll be back.

You don't doubt that for a second.

**THE END**

Everyone is holding their breath, waiting for your answer. You know, of course, that Julia and Garrett are dying to be part of the youngest team to summit Everest. You don't want to let them—or yourself—down just because you're not feeling well.

"What will it be?" Russ asks you. "Are you up to the climb today?"

"Okay," you finally say. "Let's get up to the top!"

Hans gives you a quick nod of approval, and Garrett and Julia slap you on the back. You know they're just excited, but it only makes your head throb more.

And then there's Jake, who punches your arm. "You won't regret this decision, I'm telling you!"

But you *do* regret it, and almost right away.

The wind is spitting up snow, making it impossible to see even the climber on the fixed line in front of you. It's cold and miserable. And that describes not only the weather but your own state of health as you lift one foot and dig in your crampon and then the other. Again and again, one foot, then the next, and yet you feel like you're getting nowhere.

Because today is summit day—one of the most dangerous days of the trip—the Sherpas are climbing next to their partners on the team.

Lhakpa is right behind you, and he must notice the way you're stumbling. He shouts to you, "Are you okay?"

"Yes!" you say through your oxygen mask and give him the thumbs up sign. What else can you do? Whining won't get you to the top any faster.

At one point, you catch up with Garrett. He looks like a snowman with goggles. The snow has encrusted him in a thick casing of white. And you know you must look the same.

The two of you stop for a second for a quick rest.

"How's it going?" you shout over the wind.

"Oh, great," he yells, trying to joke. "I'm just out for a little stroll in the mountains."

You try to laugh, but it takes too much energy. You keep climbing for another two hours, and then . . .

AT THE SOUTHEAST RIDGE ROCK STEPS, YOU'RE BARELY ABLE TO PUT ONE FOOT IN FRONT OF THE OTHER.

FORTUNATELY, SOMEONE IS LOOKING OUT FOR YOU.

SLIP

Your team has reached the Hillary Step. The length of a few football fields—that's all that stands between you and the summit. But the climb to this point took too long.

"It's already early afternoon, team," Russ says. "Let's not delay. The wind's picking up."

"This is the last hurdle before the summit," Doc says. "You need to be at the top of your game and really focused."

Two things you're not right now. You have to speak up.

"Russ, Doc, I don't know if I can do it," you tell them.

"I didn't come this far to turn around because of your nerves," Hans interrupts, glaring at you. He's the only one without an oxygen mask, and the uncovered skin on his face looks raw. "I intend to reach the summit today—without extra oxygen, and without you if need be."

"Okay, okay," Russ says, holding up his hands to quiet Hans. He turns to you, Garrett, and Julia. "I'll go with anyone who wants to summit. You can make up your own minds."

**IF YOU PRESS ON FOR ONE MORE HOUR TOWARD THE SUMMIT, TURN TO PAGE 153.**

**IF YOU DESCEND, TURN TO PAGE 146.**

It's not easy. Heading slowly up the mountain saps nearly every ounce of energy you've got. But finally—

"We did it!" Julia shouts through her oxygen mask. "We're the youngest team to reach the summit!"

She's right. After all the trials and effort, you've climbed to the top of Mount Everest, and the whole world is under you. Not that you can see any of it, though. You're socked in by clouds that block the views. Thick, icy snow is pelting you.

Still, Jake lets out a whoop. Hans—looking pretty near death after making the climb with no supplemental oxygen— nods his head a few times with tears in his eyes. This is the most emotion you've seen from him. Ever.

You open your mouth to join in the celebration: to tell Lhakpa you're so glad the two of you saw your shared dream of climbing the mountain come true, and to ask Dorjee Sherpa if he's changed his mind about your climbing abilities. So many things you want to say—

But guess what? There's no time.

"We've got to start our descent now," Russ announces about a minute after you arrive. "It's getting late, and there's a storm coming. Let's go."

You haven't had a chance to savor the moment. But Russ is already leading the way back across the ridge.

As you climb down the Hillary Step, Jake is above you and slips. The rope keeps him from falling too far, but he slams into your shoulder and then into the side of the steep step. Doc takes a look at you and then Jake. You're fine, but he's banged up his arm pretty good and can barely use it.

All this costs you even more time. Now you're really late. In fact, it's already getting dark.

*The sun shouldn't be setting yet.*

It's not. A storm is moving in around you, blotting out the sun and much of the light. This angry storm is mammoth, barreling down on your expedition with cutting, icy wind and vicious, blinding snow.

The blizzard is like a wedge that splits your team into two groups. Suddenly, you can't see the others in front of you. You're with Doc, Hans, Lhakpa, and Jake. But where's the rest of the team? The blowing snow has wiped out their tracks. And you stumble on, hoping to catch up with them and reach Camp Four.

"How much farther to Camp, Doc?" you shout over the wind.

"Too far!" Jake moans. "We're not going to make it!"

"We'll be okay," Doc says, but you can hear a little doubt in her voice. Two hours later, you're still wandering, lost on the mountain, and now the sun really has set. The temperature has plummeted, and you know you have frostbite on your face, hands, and toes.

"We'll stop here and dig in for the night!" Doc yells. And you try to create a snow shelter, huddling together for warmth.

"Hang in there!" Doc says. "Russ is on his way. He'll find us! Let's bet on it, okay?"

And the next morning, Russ and Dorjee *do* find you. But by then it's too late for Doc to collect on her bet. Why?

Hans, Jake, Lhakpa, Doc—and you—are all frozen solid.

**THE END**

The Death Zone.

*Good name for a bad place.*

The Death Zone is the area from Camp Four up to the summit. The air in the DZ doesn't have enough oxygen for you to survive too long. So from here on in, you'll always be wearing an oxygen mask—that is, if you want to make it to the top and get back down in one piece. Hans, as you know, has something to prove and will take his chances without supplemental oxygen.

"Today is our lucky day," Hans tells you this afternoon as you stand together on the edge of Camp Four. With a rare smile, he sweeps his arms up toward the blue sky. The weather couldn't be more clear and perfect for the start of your summit push tonight. It's just right.

Then, of course, something goes wrong.

Russ joins you two, looking tired and disappointed. "I've got bad news. The advance team that was supposed to put in the fixed ropes for our climb tonight didn't get the job done. That means there are fixed lines for only part of the route up to the summit. We'll have to wait until tomorrow—but there's no guarantee the weather will hold."

Hans is shaking his head. "You and the rest of the team might be able to wait another day, but without supplemental oxygen, I can't wait that long. I'm going tonight." Hans turns to you. "The weather is perfect! Come along with me! I'll help you get to the summit and reach your dream."

**IF YOU GO FOR THE SUMMIT WITHOUT A COMPLETE ROUTE OF FIXED ROPES, TURN TO PAGE 168.**

**IF YOU TELL HANS YOU'RE GOING TO WAIT UNTIL TOMORROW, TURN TO PAGE 185.**

Who has time for drinking more water—and a full bladder—
on a day like today?

After all, it's Summit Day, and you can't wait to get
going. As you and the team leave Camp Four that night,
you're pumped up with excitement. In just a few hours, you're
going to be at the top of the world!

That excitement fades fast, though. It's a really brutal
climb. The Hillary Step, the last big challenge before the
summit, would be an extremely tricky climb at any altitude, but
way up here it takes nearly all your strength and concentration.

You're exhausted—and cold—as you climb the long
narrow ridge that leads to the actual summit.

Then—guess what?

You made it. You're reached the top of Mount Everest!

If you weren't so tired and out of it, you'd enjoy it much
more. Garrett tries to get you to pose for a picture with him
and Julia. But you just sat down, and you've got to rest.

As the others celebrate, you try to savor the views and
catch your breath.

But before you can do either of those things, it's time to
head back down the mountain. You make your way back to
the Hillary Step. Lhakpa is sticking close to you as if he can
tell you're not doing so hot.

"You've broken your arm," Doc announces after she and Russ have examined you.

"I just wasn't thinking clearly," you say, clenching your teeth in pain. You tell them about not drinking more water at Camp Four and ask if that might've affected your climb.

"Probably," Russ says. "That's the thing about dehydration—it can make you sloppy."

Russ comes up with a plan: He will lead Garrett, Julia, Jake, and Hans back to Camp Four. Hans, who summited without supplemental oxygen, is in rough shape and needs to get down the mountain quickly. Doc and Lhakpa will help you descend.

It's slow going with your busted-up arm. As the sun sets, the temperatures drop. You can feel the cold seeping through your gloves and into your fingers. And then you can't feel them anymore.

When you finally reach Camp Four in the middle of the night, you've got frostbite on six of your fingertips. When you finally get down to Base Camp, you'll be rushed by helicopter to the hospital.

Well, at least you made the summit—and now you've got the formula for a happier climb: Just add water.

**THE END**

"Back off," you tell Hans. You reach out to push him away, but even though he's right in front of you, you miss.

"You aren't thinking straight," Hans says.

"I am so," you snap. "I just—I just—"

*I just want to ask Russ or Doc what to do.*

That's what you want to say. But you can't seem to form the words. Black curtains are closing in on your vision. Things are *really* fuzzy now. And Hans is getting even closer. This time to catch you as you start to fall off the ledge.

The last thing you hear before you black out is Hans calling for help. "Russ! Doc!"

When you come to, you're looking up into Doc's face. You're lying at the base of the Hillary Step and your head feels like someone's been using it to pound nails.

"What . . . happened?" Your words are slow and muffled through your oxygen mask.

"Your mask was blocked," Doc says. "A ball of frozen spit had formed and wouldn't let enough oxygen through. You might've died, and you're obviously still pretty weak."

*Hans was right. I need to apologize and to thank him.*

"Where's Hans?" you ask.

"He went to summit," Doc tells you. "But don't worry. Lhakpa and I are going to get you down the mountain and

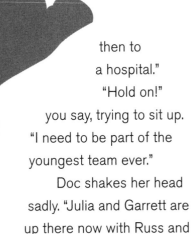

then to a hospital."

"Hold on!" you say, trying to sit up. "I need to be part of the youngest team ever."

Doc shakes her head sadly. "Julia and Garrett are up there now with Russ and the others. It's too late and you don't have the strength anyway. I'm sorry."

You turn to Lhakpa, who is standing next to Doc. "But, Lhakpa, it was your dream to summit, too."

Lhakpa explains that he could've gone up if he wanted, but he chose to stay with you. "It's not meant to be this year for either of us," he says. "Maybe in the future we can reach our goal together."

You feel the truth sink in. Your dream is over—for now anyway. You thank Lhakpa and shake his hand.

"Okay," you finally say. "I'm ready. Let's head down."

*THE END*

You guzzle another liter of water. But it's no treat.

Before you know it, Russ is calling everyone to meet outside his tent. You feel like you should say something important to Julia and Garrett, to thank them for waiting for you when you decided not to summit yesterday. But with the oxygen mask on your mouth, there's not a lot you can say. So you just nod at each of them, and they nod back.

Then your climb begins.

If all goes well, it should take you about ten hours to reach the summit from Camp Four. But you wonder if it will actually take six days. Each step is *very* slow and seems to take so much energy.

For the first time, the Sherpas are climbing next to each member of the team.  At one point, Lhakpa turns to you and gives you a thumbs-up.

"Stay focused," he says.

Good advice. The thinnest air yet, strong winds, and tricky climbing conditions can lead to really bad decisions. Accidents can easily happen here. The lethal kind.

Just then, your team reaches the Hillary Step.

THE HILLARY STEP. THE LAST OBSTACLE BEFORE THE SUMMIT.

WHEN GARRETT SLIPS...

LHAKPA GOES AHEAD TO HELP.

NOW IT'S JUST YOU AND HANS.

You give Hans a thumbs-up, trying to be positive.

"We're not there yet!" Hans says. Without an oxygen mask, he's really gasping for air.

For some reason, the word *yet* runs through your suddenly aching head. And that makes you think of *yeti*. Not that you believe in abominable snowmen. That's just silly.

"Do you believe in monsters, Hans?" you ask, taking your mask off your mouth.

Hans cocks his head. "What?"

"You know, like the abdominal yeti," you say.

"Are you okay?" Hans asks.

"I'm fine," you say. Whoa. That was freaky. Your mind drifted off about yetis for a second. But now you're back.

"Put your mask back on," Hans says. "Hurry."

Hans leans closer. Too close.

*Where's Russ? Where's Doc?*

You step back. But there's nowhere to go but down.

"Stop," Hans says. "Stop moving."

"Sharks don't," you say, putting the mask back on.

Hans does a double take. "You're not making sense. Let me check the oxygen flow to your mask."

You bat his hand away. Hans looks surprised. "I'm trying to help you."

*Help? Or steal my oxygen? Hans knows he can't make it without oxygen—now he wants mine!*

"Get back!" you shout.

"I want to help you," Hans says. "Will you let me?"

He reaches for your mask a second time. Instinctively, you stop him again. Without oxygen, you won't last long up here.

"Trust me," he says, his voice sounding hoarse.

**IF YOU LET HANS LOOK AT YOUR MASK, TURN TO PAGE 173.**

**IF YOU REFUSE TO LET HANS LOOK AT YOUR MASK, TURN TO PAGE 162.**

THAT NIGHT, HANS LEADS YOU TO THE SUMMIT.

SO FAR, SO GOOD. PLENTY OF FIXED ROPES.

THERE IT IS — THE SUMMIT! AT THE END OF THE RIDGE.

NO FIXED LINES HERE — BUT YOU CAN DO IT!

On a scale of one to ten, it's a choice with a difficulty rating of, oh, about eighteen. But you're glad to be at Camp Four later when a terrifying storm strikes.

Lhakpa, your Sherpa climbing partner for summit day, stands next to you as you scan the mountain for any sign of your teammates, who all decided to summit. Not going to happen. The blowing snow and approaching nightfall have made it nearly impossible to see past your hand in front of your face.

"You respected the mountain!" Lhakpa shouts over the screaming wind. "You listened to your instincts and made the right decision!"

"Thanks!" you say, looking up at the darkening sky. "But I'm worried about the others! And the sun is setting!"

Five hours later, in the pitch darkness, your team starts to trickle into camp. It's like they've just returned from some violent war. They're limping and coughing, and they look near death. The only ones who look in semi-decent shape are Hans, Doc, and Russ.

Julia lost her goggles in a fall early on and is now snow-blind. On top of that, her fingers and toes are severely frostbitten.

It's Jake who's in the worst shape, though. His night on the mountain has taken its toll. His face is black with frostbite, and he's done something to his ankle. It's not broken, but he can barely put weight on it. He's going to need two people—one on either side—to walk him down, planting each and every step for him.

"We were close," Russ tells you, "but we didn't reach the summit. The storm pushed us back, and by then it was too late to make it back here in daylight."

The other teams who tried to summit have taken a beating too. Thirty climbers are hurt or missing.

That morning, your team somehow makes its way down to Camp Three. There, Russ and Doc come up with a plan of action. First, they ask many of your team's Sherpas to help injured climbers from other teams who don't have enough Sherpas on their expeditions. Second, Doc gets ready to lead the still-blinded Julia down the mountain. And finally, Russ talks to Hans and you about bringing Jake down to Base Camp, where a helicopter can pick him up.

But Jake won't have it. "Finish the climb," he rasps to you and Hans.

Hans looks at him. "Are you sure, Jake?"

"I paid for the trip in more ways than one," Jake answers, pointing a blackened hand toward his blackened face. "If you go down now, that's it. There won't be any more climbing days this season."

Then he turns to you.

"Besides, you're not a rescue professional. You're a climber," Jake says. "Leave it to the pros to help me, and you go summit this mountain. Do it for all of us."

Russ, Jake, and Hans talk quietly for a moment. When they're done, Russ says to you. "Okay, Hans is going to hook up with another team at Camp Four in the morning and push for the summit tomorrow night. If you decide you want to summit, too, I'll go with you guys. I promised your family I'd stick with you."

*Wow, I could reach the summit after all!*

"If you decide not to go," Russ continues, "you can give Lhakpa a hand getting Jake down the mountain. And I can help climbers from other teams who are hurt."

What will it be?

IF YOU LET GO OF YOUR DREAM TO SUMMIT THIS YEAR AND HELP JAKE DESCEND, TURN TO PAGE 180.

IF YOU DECIDE TO PUSH FOR THE SUMMIT, TURN TO PAGE 157.

You slip off the mask quickly—and the wind and snow and cold attack your exposed skin. It's like sticking your face out of a moving plane.

"Hurry," you manage to croak. "Please."

Moving fast, Hans knocks the mask with his hand. Nothing. He knocks again, and—

*Pop!*

A chunk of ice falls out. Your spit must have formed an ice ball. It had been clogging your mask and blocking the oxygen. Hans shoves the mask at you, and you put it back on.

The whole process takes about ten seconds. And it saves your life.

"Thanks, Hans," you say as sweet, sweet oxygen flows into your lungs.

It's like someone has lifted a heavy weight off your body. Without oxygen, you'd been weak and slow. Every step and every breath had been a struggle. And it wasn't just your body—your mind had been affected, too. You were going nutty, seeing and thinking things that weren't real or true. But now you can think more clearly again.

Together, you and Hans finish scaling the Hillary Step. The others are waiting for you.

"Homestretch," Hans rasps.

And he's right. You're very close to the summit now.

JUST... ONE... MORE...
STEP... AND...

"You did it!" says Russ, giving you a hug. Doc joins in, and soon, the whole team is in one big hug.

In a flash, you flip through images of the last few weeks. Scary times like the landing in Lukla and the dreaded Khumbu Icefall. But also the fun—laughing with Garrett and Julia, the soccer match, and getting to know Lhakpa.

You've heard that climbers and Sherpas form lifelong bonds. And now you can see why. This experience has welded you and Lhakpa together.

"You were right, Lhakpa," you tell him. "Together we reached our dream."

Dorjee walks over to you. The sirdar gives you one of his nods. And then with a smile that could power a small city, he throws his arms around you. "Congratulations," he tells you.

You pose for a picture with Garrett and Julia. Jake has a banner in his pack, and he gives it to you to hold for the photo. It shows the logo of his video game company.

But something in Jake has changed. As if thinking better of it, he takes the banner back and says, "The picture should just be of the three of you!"

*Click!* Smile. *Click!* Smile. You take tons of pictures. Now, to enjoy the view some more—

"We still need to get down in one piece and should get

going," Doc says. Then when everyone moans, Doc adds with a laugh, "Okay, okay. Let's just hang out for a bit."

You stay at the top for about fifteen minutes. It's not long, considering the time it took you to get there. But your bodies are getting weaker by the second up here.

Pumped up by your accomplishment, you make your way back down Mount Everest. When you reach Base Camp two days later, you can see the reporters and camera crews already there, waiting to talk to you and the rest of the team.

And, wow, do you have a story to tell!

It's kind of like working with a puppet—a very heavy one. Jake is so weak that you and Lhakpa have to move his legs for him as you help him descend the mountain.

If Jake's injuries were life threatening, a helicopter could pick him up on a clear day at Camp Two. That's very dangerous, though—a helicopter's blades have trouble lifting the craft in the thin air, and the pilot could easily lose control and crash.

So, since Jake's condition is stable, even though he's a wreck, you and Lhakpa have to help him all the way back down to Base Camp.

With you and Lhakpa on either side, each step you plant

for Jake takes time. Luckily, the sky has cleared, and Jake keeps everyone's spirits up with a corny knock-knock joke every now and then. You can see why he runs such a cool video game company—he's sort of a big kid himself.

When you reach the helicopter landing pad at Base Camp, you can barely stay standing, you're so tired. Even Lhakpa, who is more used to hard climbs and high altitudes, looks beat.

"Thank you," Jake says to you and Lhakpa, tears forming in his eyes as the medics strap him into the helicopter. "I'm glad you chose to help me."

"No problem," you tell him. "It was the right thing to do."

"I've got two pieces of news for you," Jake says. "You'll both be getting free video games for the rest of your lives. And, better yet, I'll be sponsoring another Everest trip for you and Lhakpa next year."

"Can we include Russ and Doc as guides if they can do it?" you ask. "And Hans, Garrett, and Julia, too?"

Jake smiles. "It can be the exact same team if you want. I think I'll even come along again."

Minutes later, you and Lhakpa watch the helicopter lift off and then start your way down to Base Camp. You're already looking forward to next year. Why?

That's when your dream of reaching the summit will come true!

**THE END**

It's the perfect day to summit. Well, at least in terms of the sunny, clear weather.

When it comes to the number of people up here—well, that's not so good.

"Holy cow," you say when you see the backup of climbers at the southeast ridge rock steps.

As you wait, you lose precious time. If it gets too late, you'll probably have to turn around—you don't want to be stuck coming down from the summit in the dark. And are those storm clouds forming in the distance heading your way?

Finally, though, it's your turn. Once Russ leads you through, you pick up speed and make up some time. Then—

*Oh no.*

There's another bottleneck of climbers at the Hillary Step! This steep wall is the last challenge before the summit. You're so close. But you have to wait your turn.

Again.

Time is running out. If you keep going, you run the risk of having to climb back down in the dark. Then again, the climbing season is ending soon, and this may be your only chance to summit this year.

**IF YOU KEEP CLIMBING TOWARD THE SUMMIT FOR ONE MORE HOUR, TURN TO PAGE 153.**

**IF YOU GIVE UP ON THE SUMMIT AND HEAD BACK TO CAMP FOUR, TURN TO PAGE 170.**

"Climbing without fixed ropes in the Death Zone?" you say. "That's a *really* bad idea, Hans. Count me out."

Russ nods in approval and so does the rest of the team. Not Hans, though. He's determined to climb anyway and starts collecting his gear for his push to the summit.

But then Russ says, "It's not going to happen, Hans."

"What do you mean?" Hans rasps. "I'll just go up on my own and meet you back here or at Camp Three."

"No," Russ says. "I don't want you to go alone, especially since you're not on supplemental oxygen. Splitting up now could be a disaster. We'll have another chance next week."

Hans's face, already splotchy from lack of oxygen and the cold, gets even redder with anger. He points at you and snaps at Russ, "We're going to let a *kid* tell us what to do?"

"In this case," Russ says, "absolutely."

In the end, Hans agrees to descend with the rest of you. As the lead guide, Russ is running the show and Hans really doesn't have a choice. But that doesn't mean he's forgiven you. All the way back to Base Camp, Hans gives you the silent treatment and shoots you furious looks.

A week later, it's bad news. The weather's turned sour at the summit, and there won't be any more climbing this season. You've missed your chance to reach the top of the world this year. It's rough, especially after how hard you worked. The plan now is to hike back to Lukla and start the journey home.

After you've said good-bye to Lhakpa—you're going to write him and meet up again when you come back to summit someday—Dorjee Sherpa asks to speak with you.

Dorjee gives you a long look. "I think you've learned a lot on your trip to Everest, haven't you?"

"I hope so," you say. "Maybe I've learned what it means to make the right decisions."

"Yes, you did," he says. "I was very impressed."

Then Dorjee gives you a smile and a high five.

"Oh, please," Hans, who's walking nearby, says sarcastically. He's still upset about your choice not to climb without fixed ropes.

*Let him stew*, you think. Something tells you that you might have saved his life.——

THE END

HEY THERE,

WE'VE PUT TOGETHER THESE MATERIALS SO YOU CAN GET TOTALLY PREPPED AND REVVED UP FOR EVEREST.

SEE YOU IN KATHMANDU!
— RUSS AND DOC

EXPEDITION FILE:
# EVEREST

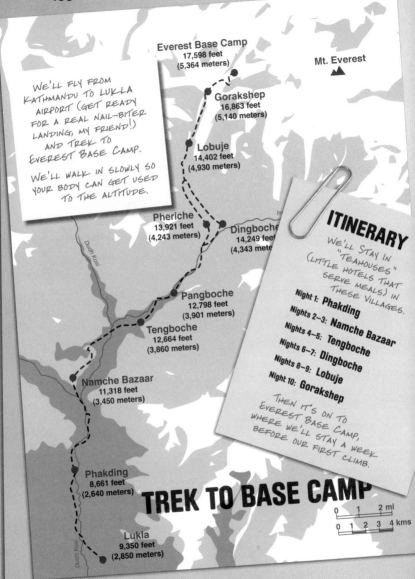

*Lukla airport*

*Namche Bazaar*

*Yaks carry loads on Everest expeditions.*

*Porters carry loads in cone-shaped baskets called* dokos.

# PEOPLE AND CULTURE ALONG THE WAY

On your trek, you'll pass through lots of villages, try new foods, hear new languages, visit sacred places, and much more. It's an adventure in itself—before you even get to the base of Everest! This is just a taste to get you ready.

## Foods

***Dal bhat*** (pronounced "doll bot") is the local meal of choice. It's rice, lentils, and a vegetable on the side. Your best bet for fresh, safe food is to eat like the locals do.

You'll see **yak** steak on the menu at the local teahouse restaurants. This is not actually yak meat—it's water buffalo raised in lower altitudes.

You'll see bakery goods like **apple pie** for sale at villages, made especially for foreigners. Be careful—bakery items often don't cook completely at high altitude, so they can carry a lot of bacteria (probably from the baker's hands) that can give you food poisoning.

EVEREST BY ANOTHER NAME—

THE SHERPA NAME:
CHOMOLUNGMA

THE NEPALESE NAME:
SAGARMATHA

## Sacred Flags and Wheels

These are prayer wheels. People turn them clockwise when they walk past them to "say" the prayer.

Prayer flags have prayers printed on them and are hung on stone shrines called *stupas* and on mountaintops. Buddhists believe that when the flags flap in the breeze, blessings are carried across the countryside.

## How to Say Hello in Nepal

When you pass Nepali people on the trail between villages, here's how to greet them. They will often greet you like this.

1. Press your hands together and hold them just below your chin.

2. Bow your head a little.

3. Say *Namaste* (NAH-mah-stay).

    This means, "I salute the god in you." If you want to show respect (to an older or very important person), say *Namaskar* instead.

# THE ROUTE TO THE TOP OF THE WORLD

Mt. Everest Summit
29,029 feet
(8,848 meters)

Camp 4
26,300 feet
(8,016 meters)

Camp 3
23,500 feet
(7,163 meters)

Camp 2
21,000 feet
(6,401 meters)

Camp 1
19,500 feet
(5,944 meters)

The Khumbu
Icefall

Base Camp
17,598 feet
(5,364 meters)

THE ITINERARY WILL PROBABLY CHANGE DEPENDING ON THE WEATHER, THE CONDITIONS ON THE MOUNTAIN, AND HOW EVERYONE'S FEELING.

THIS IS JUST TO GIVE YOU AN IDEA OF WHAT TO EXPECT.

## DAY    EXPEDITION ITINERARY

GOING DOWN LOWER WILL GIVE YOUR
BODY A REST FROM THE EXTREME
ALTITUDE SO YOU'LL BE STRONGER
FOR THE SUMMIT PUSH.

| DAY | |
|---|---|
| 1–2 | Fly from home to Bangkok, Thailand |
| 3 | Fly from Bangkok to Kathmandu, Nepal |
| 4 | Tour Kathmandu |
| 5 | Fly to Lukla, Nepal |
| 6–16 | Trek to Base Camp (BC) |
| 17–20 | Rest in BC, organize, set up, skills review |
| 21 | Puja ceremony |
| 22 | Climb through icefall to 19,000 feet (5,791 meters), return to BC. |
| 23 | Climb to Camp I (CI), overnight CI |
| 24 | Climb toward Camp II (CII), return CI, overnight CI |
| 25 | Return to BC |
| 26–28 | Rest BC |
| 29 | Climb to CI, overnight CI |
| 30 | Climb to CII, overnight CII |
| 31 | Rest CII, overnight CII |
| 32 | Climb to base of Lhotse Face, return CII, overnight CII |
| 33 | Return to BC |
| 34–36 | Rest BC |
| 37 | Climb to CII, overnight CII |
| 38 | Rest CII, overnight CII |
| 39 | Climb to Camp III (CIII), overnight CIII |
| 40 | Return to CII, overnight CII |
| 41 | Return to BC |
| 42 | Drop below BC to Pheriche, overnight in Pheriche |
| 43 | Pheriche to Pangboche, overnight in Pangboche |
| 44 | Overnight in Pangboche |
| 45 | Overnight in Pangboche |
| 46 | Return to BC from Pangboche |
| 47–49 | Rest BC, wait for good forecast |
| 50 | Climb to CII, overnight CII |
| 51 | Rest CII, overnight CII |
| 52 | Climb to CIII, overnight CIII |
| 53 | Climb to Camp IV (CIV), overnight CIV |
| | Leave for summit attempt at 10 p.m. in the evening of Day 53 |
| 54 | Summit around 8 a.m., return to CIV, overnight CIV |
| 55 | Return to CII, overnight CII |
| 56 | Return to BC, overnight BC |
| 57 | Leave BC |

SHORT TRIPS LIKE THIS GET YOUR
BODY USED TO THE HIGH ALTITUDE.
WE'LL DO A LOT OF 'EM!

MOST OF THE CLIMB IS IN
THE DARK. DON'T FORGET
YOUR HEADLAMP!

# Gear Checklist

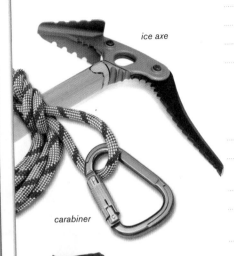

*ice axe*

*carabiner*

CHECK THE FIT
OF YOUR LAYERED
SOCKS INSIDE
YOUR BOOTS.

TOO TIGHT =
REDUCED BLOOD
FLOW IN YOUR FEET,
WHICH CAN CAUSE
FROSTBITE.

*climbing boots*

*crampons*

## Climbing Equipment

Ice axe with leash

Crampons

Carabiners (six)

Climbing harness

WE'LL HAVE EVERYTHING
ELSE YOU NEED.

## Clothing

Lightweight long underwear

Heavyweight long underwear

Down-filled expedition
parka with hood

Down-filled pants

Waterproof, breathable
jacket and pants

Short-sleeve shirt

Lightweight nylon pants

## Footwear

Hiking boots for the trek
to Base Camp

Trekking socks

Plastic climbing boots
with liners

Liner socks

Wool socks to wear
over liner socks

Camp booties to wear in tent

Gaiters

## Hand Wear

Lightweight synthetic gloves

Heavyweight synthetic gloves

Expedition shell gloves with removable liners

Hand warmers and toe warmers

## Head Wear

Ski goggles

Glacier glasses

Headlamp for night climbs and nighttime camp use

Baseball cap or any hat with visor for camp use

Wool hat

Face masks—lightweight and heavyweight

## Personal Equipment

Expedition backpack

Expedition sleeping bag for nights on the mountain (rated to at least −40°F (−40°C)

Expedition sleeping bag for nights at base camp (rated to at least −20°F (−30°C)

Self-inflating pad for sleeping on

Foam pad for sleeping on

Cup

Bowl

Spoon

Camp knife

Water bottles

Pee bottle for use in tent. A regular water bottle will do— but mark it clearly!

Girls: Pee funnel so you can pee in the bottle (practice at home!)

Sunscreen

Lip balm with sunscreen

*ski goggles*

*glacier glasses*

# How to Fend Off Frostbite

Aside from wearing the right clothes to stay warm, what else can you do to prevent your flesh from freezing?

### Free your feet

Cold feet just need another layer of socks, right? Not necessarily. If you pile on too many socks and make your boots too tight, you'll restrict the flow of warm blood in your feet. That's a recipe for toe-sicles. So, keep your feet unsqueezed and wiggle your toes every so often to keep the blood flowing.

### Watch for waxy spots

When frostbite starts to set in, you'll see small patches of waxy, whitish skin. They'll feel firm and numb. Exposed areas of the face—particularly the nose and ears—and hands are most at risk. Check your companions' faces and ask them to check yours. If you find a numb spot, place a warm body part on it and apply pressure. Just don't rub, as that could damage the tissue.

## If you do get frostbite . . .

**1** ### Keep it frozen

Once your flesh is frozen, the damage has been done, and keeping it frozen won't make it worse. But if the flesh thaws and refreezes, you'll have more damage for sure. Also, infection can set in if you unfreeze the flesh in non-sterile conditions. So, keep the flesh frozen until you *know* you can safely unfreeze.

**2** ### Thaw in warm water

To thaw the frozen flesh, soak it in warm water that's kept at a temperature of 104°F (40°C) to 108°F (42°C) until the flesh is pink again. **Warning:** This will hurt. A lot.

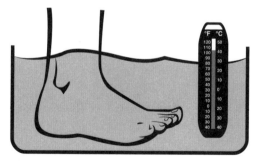

## Wise Ways to Stay Warm

### Wear layers.

Your body heat warms a thin layer of air next to your skin. Keep that "blanket" of air around you by wearing layers to trap it.

### Cover your head, neck, and hands.

These areas have blood vessels that come very close to the surface of the body, so you lose a lot of heat through these parts if they're not covered.

### Sit on an insulating pad.

Sitting on cold ground or ice will suck the warmth right out of you.

### Cover your mouth.

Cover your mouth with a wool or fleece mouth covering to avoid losing heat each time you exhale. This also warms the air you breathe *in* so you don't lose heat in your lungs.

### Eat foods high in carbohydrates.

Your body can turn these quickly and easily into heat for your cold body.

# How to Survive an Ice Avalanche

The best way to survive an ice avalanche is not to be there when one happens. That means, don't climb through the Khumbu Icefall in the late afternoon when the sun is hot and ice is melting and collapsing. But if you find yourself in the icefall at just the wrong moment, here's what to do.

### If there is shelter nearby, unclip and hide behind it.

A giant serac (a column of ice) in an icefall can be your best friend. Or at least a shield from incoming blocks of ice.
**Be Aware:** If the serac is dripping wet or already leaning precariously, it's probably unstable, so avoid it. It could collapse on you.

### If there is nowhere to hide and the avalanche is coming right at you, stay clipped in.

If you survive the impact of all those blocks of ice hurtling at you, rescuers will hopefully be able to find you by following the rope.

### Kneel down and cover your head with your arms.

And hope for the best.

# How NOT to Fall into a Crevasse

A crevasse is a giant crack in a glacier. Crevasses can be as deep as 100 feet (30 meters), and they have nearly vertical walls of solid ice. Not a place you want to be! Here's how to stay out.

## Stay clipped to a fixed rope.

A fixed rope (attached to the snow and ice with anchors) is your best friend when climbing through a glacier or icefall. Use it. Even when you take a bathroom break.

**Be Aware:** You will have to cross ladder bridges over crevasses in the Khumbu Icefall. During these crossings, if you become unstable, lean forward to make the fixed rope taut. This will help stabilize you.

### If there are no fixed ropes, rope up with your fellow climbers.

Then one of them can hopefully stop your fall or pull you out—and you can be ready to do the same for them.

### Don't wander in a whiteout.

In whiteout conditions, if you can't clip to a fixed rope that leads you right back to camp, try to stay put until the snowstorm clears, assuming you have all the gear and supplies you need. Trying to walk in the blind can easily get you "crevassed"—or lost.

### Be especially careful the morning after a snowfall.

Even a light snow can temporarily cover a crevasse, creating a weak snow bridge that will collapse when you step on it. So, when there's fresh snow, definitely rope up.

# How to Avoid Altitude Sickness

**1** **Climb slowly.**

Your body needs time to adjust to the "thin air" (air has less oxygen the higher you go). By taking it slow, you're giving your body time to make more red blood cells that can carry more oxygen.

**2** **Have "rest" days.**

Schedule some rest days during your climb, when you stay at a certain altitude to give your body time to adjust. Keep in mind: A "rest day" doesn't mean you have to sit around or sleep all day. Go for an easy stroll if you're feeling up to it. Mild exercise may help your body adapt.

**3** **Stop ascent if symptoms develop.**

Symptoms of mild altitude sickness include exhaustion, headache, nausea, lack of appetite, and shortness of breath. If you feel any or all of these, stop ascent, take your team doctor's recommended medicine for the headache, make an effort to breathe deeply and regularly, and drink plenty of fluids.

**4** **Descend if symptoms continue.**

If you don't feel better after twenty-four hours, descend immediately and get medical attention.

**Be Aware:** These two very serious conditions can result from ascending too fast and ignoring the symptoms of altitude sickness:

## HACE (High-Altitude Cerebral Edema):

This happens when the brain swells at high altitude. Symptoms include severe headache, nausea, confusion, and difficulty with walking and balance.

## HAPE (High-Altitude Pulmonary Edema):

This happens when fluid leaks into the lungs at high altitude. Symptoms include a hacking cough and later, shortness of breath and dizziness.

Both conditions can be fatal and require **immediate descent.**

## Other High-Altitude Hazards

It's easy to get dehydrated at high altitudes because the air is so dry. On summit day, drink at least two liters of water before the climb, three liters of water during the climb, and two liters after the climb.

At Camp Three and above, the air is so thin that you'll need supplemental oxygen. If you start to feel short of breath, dizzy, or confused, check the oxygen valve and mask to make sure the oxygen is flowing.

Sunlight reflecting off the ice on the mountain can sunburn the surface of your eye—a very painful condition called *snow blindness.* To prevent it, always wear UV-light-blocking sunglasses with side shields (glacier glasses) or goggles.

# ABOUT THE CONTRIBUTORS

## AUTHORS

**Bill Doyle** is proud that he managed to write about the dangerous climb up Mount Everest without getting frostbite or falling into a crevasse. He lives in New York City. Visit him online at billdoyle.net.

**David Borgenicht** is the co-author of all the books in the "Worst-Case Scenario" series. He lives in Philadelphia.

## CLIMBING CONSULTANT

**David Morton** has reached the summit of Everest six times and is one of the premier international expedition leaders operating today. In addition to Everest, David has guided the Seven Summits (the highest peak on each continent) and climbed extensively throughout the world. He lives in Seattle.

## ILLUSTRATOR

**Yancey Labat** got his start with Marvel Comics and has since been illustrating children's books. He lives in New York.

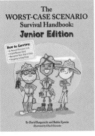